Norman Rockwell's Greatest Painting

Previous novels by Hollis Hodges

The Fabricator. N.Y. 1976
Don't Tell Me Your Name. N.Y. 1978

Norman Rockwell's Greatest Painting

A Novel

HOLLIS HODGES

PAUL S. ERIKSSON, *Publisher*
Middlebury, Vermont

Manufactured in the United States of America

10 9 8 7 6 5 4 3 2 1

Library of Congress Cataloging-in-Publication Data

Hodges, Hollis.
     Norman Rockwell's greatest painting : a novel / by Hollis Hodges.
          p.   cm.
     ISBN 0-8397-6405-7 : $16.95
     1. Rockwell, Norman, 1894-1978--Fiction.   I. Title.
PS3558.O3434N67 1988
813'.54--dc19   88-11022
                                                          CIP

To the People of Stockbridge

Any resemblance of characters in this novel to persons living or dead is purely coincidental.

None of you are in this book. The only real character I used was Norman Rockwell, and he is no longer with us. I even tried to avoid using the name of anyone in our area. Nothing here is meant to portray Stockbridge in any but a favorable light. It is a good town to live in or visit. Great place to raise kids.

There is, of course, no such painting as *The Honeymooners*. What Norman Rockwell's greatest painting is, I do not know.

— Hollis Hodges
Stockbridge, Mass

To Harold, Itsy, John, Howard, and Hubie. To their spouses, their offspring, and their offspring's offspring.

To Vincent Van Gogh, who painted what he wanted to paint the way he wanted to paint it, and during his lifetime never sold a painting.

...and to the woman who wrote me that nice letter of only two sentences: "The next time you write a book, may I live in it. Thank you."

I said yes, of course.

Everyone has a story.

— Marilyn

Norman Rockwell's Greatest Painting

One

People who tour the Norman Rockwell Museum in Stockbridge, Massachusetts, find that when they leave the building and walk down Main Street many people seem to look familiar. These are faces they had seen only moments ago in a Norman Rockwell painting. This is because the tour guide always mentions that Rockwell used local people for his models, and that many of them still live in town. The boy who modeled for the painting in the doctor's office, for instance, now owns a hardware store or construction company. And the man who modeled for the salesman now owns a garage or real estate office, or something. So, if the tourist fresh from the museum happens to see someone who looks as if he might have modeled for a Norman Rockwell painting, sometimes they ask if he will let them take his picture. It makes a nice souvenir.

That happened to Olney once when he and the girls were in town on their way to get ice cream cones. Two middle-aged women coming from the museum looked at Olney, then at one another, stopped and asked if he would mind if they took his picture.

It might be that this had nothing at all to do with Rockwell. It might only have been that he and the girls made an interesting-looking little group. The big balding man, the tall teenage black girl holding a basketball, and the short chubby ten-year-old carrying a small sketch pad and a few pencils. With a friendly-looking medium-size black dog walking in front of them

Olney, said all right, of course.

"But I think the girls and my dog should be in the picture, too."

Of course. That was what they had had in mind.

Cheryl and Heather looked at one another and shook their heads.

"Oh, Olney."

He said, "It's all right. It won't take long. Just stand still and smile."

They did. The ladies said, "Thank you." Olney said, "You're welcome," and that was that.

Cheryl said, "Olney, you're funny."

He denied that.

He said, "All we did was take a few moments to do something that made a couple nice ladies happy. And didn't cost anything."

He said, "Whenever you can do something to please someone and it doesn't cost anything, do it. Sometimes even if it does."

The kids shook their heads again.

Heather bounced her basketball on the sidewalk a few times.

Olney, sixty-five years old, five feet eleven, broad, a bit overweight, had the relaxed and roughened face of a retired working man. He had brown eyes and somewhat curly black hair, some strands of which he combed across the top of his head to cover a bald spot. Not that a little baldness mattered that much, of course. But he did it anyway.

Olney had been born and raised over in Northampton, about forty-five miles from Stockbridge. Two years ago he and his wife had moved here and bought a big old corner house on the corner of South and Clark Streets and converted it into a building of four apartments. It had been a big gray eyesore and badly run down because the people who had owned it had long ago lost interest in its condition or appearance. Olney and his wife built a screened porch across the front of the house, a wide wooden deck in back, and planted flowers and shrubs and a few small trees. And painted it yellow with blue shutters. Some of the neighbors thought that color scheme a bit too much, but everyone agreed that it was a great improvement over what had been there before.

Olney lived in one apartment and rented out the other three.

Olney had a few brothers and sisters scattered around the country, his dog, Solomon, a rowboat he kept at Bill's Bait Shop over at Laurel Lake in Lee, a daughter in northern California and a son in Los Angeles. Both were married and had three children.

He used to have an outboard motorboat parked on a carrier out beside the garage and next to that a medium-size camper. He had sold both a year ago because they weren't fun anymore.

Perhaps that had been a bit hasty, but it was what he felt like doing at the time, so he had done it. Sold the motorboat and carrier cheap to an old friend over in Northampton, and sold the camper back to the man he'd bought it from.

He didn't use the screened porch in front much anymore. Mostly he sat on the deck in back. There were tables and chairs there and an outdoor grill. Off to one side was the garage with a basketball net and backboard above the doors. Toward the back of the lot was a medium-size garden, and beyond that a good view of the green Berkshire hills.

His full name was Ebert Olney.

Ebert had been the name of his mother's favorite uncle, who had died just before Olney had been born. He never used the name Ebert. He always told people his name was Olney. He wanted people to call him that.

Late one night a little less than a year and a half ago a young doctor inexperienced at this kind of thing had hesitatingly put an arm on Olney's shoulder and broken the news that his wife had died.

Only an hour ago he had said that she was holding her own. Maybe even showing some improvement. Olney reminded him of that.

"I'm sorry. But there was nothing anyone could do."

"I don't believe that."

"It's true. We all did everything we could do."

The young doctor looked as if he had already cried. And might do so again at any moment.

He and the young doctor looked at one another for several long moments. Then Olney turned and walked out.

That was that.

There had been nothing anyone could do.

He left the hospital and walked the streets and thought about it. That was late January. The snow had stopped and had been replaced by bitter winds that drove home the point that life was hard and cruel. Which it was. Olney agreed with that. He walked a long time, then finally stopped and sat on a low stone wall in front of someone's house and took off his coat and hat and unbuttoned his shirt and thought how nice it would be to just sit there and freeze to death.

Which didn't happen, of course.

Later, when it began to get light, he walked back to the hospital parking lot, got into his car and went home to phone the kids in California and tell them that their mother had died and there hadn't been anything anyone could do.

At first he thought of selling the house and moving back to Northampton, where he had friends, then changed his mind. He finished converting the house into apartments. Settled in. Spent a lot of time in back drinking beer and smoking cigars. Had some good times and some bad times. Some winning and some losing. Nothing that a retired plumber with a lot of patience and a sense of humor couldn't handle.

Stockbridge, population two thousand, three hundred and seventy-nine, is in Berkshire County in western Massachusetts. To many people across the country this small village is the personification of small-town America. Main Street is only one block long. At one end is the stately Red Lion Inn, which has held that position for over two hundred years. On the long porch guests sip drinks and watch tourists and townspeople pass by. And vice versa. And at the other end, past shops and stores and the bank and the small art gallery, is the library. A brick structure nicely landscaped and quietly fitting for a town of wealth, culture, and intellect. And across from the library is the Norman Rockwell Museum.

It is during the summertime that the area comes alive. The Boston Symphony plays at Tanglewood for nine weeks and the best modern dance and jazz in the country can be found at Jacob's Pillow. There is the Shakespeare Theater Festival, the Berkshire Playhouse, and Chesterwood, the former home and studio of the great sculptor Daniel Chester French. And overlooking Stockbridge Bowl is a small red house where Nathaniel Hawthorne wrote *The House of the Seven Gables*.

There is much more, of course. The area is replete with sites and scenes of historic interest. Every summer day brings hundreds of cars and busses filled with people drawn to the village by one attraction or another. Everyone, of course, tries to get a parking spot in front of the Red Lion Inn or one of the three parking spaces in front of the post office on Elm Street.

The most important thing of all, however, is this: Regardless of the many attractions the area offers, when people think of Stockbridge they think of it as the place where Norman Rockwell lived and worked and died. More than a hundred thousand people a year pass through the Norman Rockwell Museum. They come from every state in the union to stand in front of his paintings and marvel at them and tell one another that no painter anywhere has been able to capture the spirit of America the way Rockwell did.

And they are right.

Many famous people have walked down Main Street in Stockbridge, but the sentimental favorite of all time, without question, is Norman Rockwell. His influence on the community has been deep and permanent.

One writer, in a widely read article in *The Atlantic* many years ago, phrased it this way:

"Stockbridge is nothing but one big Norman Rockwell fan club."

Olney stayed in town long enough to get to know why the people felt that way. Being a bit on the sentimental side himself, he fit right in. He even got heavily involved with a number of people who had modeled for one of Norman Rockwell's best known paintings.

Olney sat on the deck behind the house, enjoying the afternoon sun and watching Heather throwing a basketball at the net he had installed above the garage door. Closer, half a dozen feet away, Cheryl was kneeling on a pad Olney had gotten for her, her sketch pad on top of the table in front of her, occasionally making a line or two and then looking up. And Solomon sprawled next to her not doing much of anything.

A few weeks ago, not long after school was out for the summer, the kids were passing the house one morning and Solomon, wagging his tail, had gone out to get acquainted. They had followed him back up the driveway, Heather bouncing her basketball and Cheryl clutching her sketch pad. They told Olney they lived at the other end of the street and thought they'd stop and say hello.

They were an improbable-looking pair.

Cheryl, ten years old, short and chubby, brown hair, large brown eyes and a serious look on her face. And Heather, thirteen, tall, black, thick dark frizzly hair, with a cautious and hesitant smile. As if she were not sure the smile would be returned.

Olney invited them to sit down, then went inside and got a couple Cokes for them and a beer and cigar for himself. And they sat and talked for a while.

Cheryl planned to be a cartoonist when she grew up. And Heather thought maybe she could someday be the first woman to play for the Boston Celtics.

The problem was that Heather had no place to practice and Cheryl didn't have anyone willing to sit still long enough for her to sketch them. So Olney bought a basketball hoop and backboard the next day and put that up on the front of the garage. That solved Heather's problem. And because lots of afternoons Olney didn't have much to do except sit on the deck and have a beer and a cigar and maybe listen to a ballgame on the radio, Cheryl's problem was taken care of.

Cheryl said, "You're moving again."

"Sorry. I was watching Heather."

She said, "Try not to move so much."

A little later, she said, "Now look straight ahead."
So he did that.

She and Olney were working on a book of cartoons. They talked sometimes about what they were going to do with all the money they would have when the cartoon book was published and they were famous. Cheryl had in mind maybe getting a big house with a swimming pool and a tennis court. Olney said most likely he would just keep on living here but buy imported beer and expensive cigars.

Heather made a basket from a long way out, and Olney risked moving just a little so he could call out, "Good shot."

She said, "Thank you."

Then she decided to rest for a while, came over and sat down. Resting the basketball in her lap.

"I'd get you a Coke," Olney said, "but I'm not allowed to move."

He suggested she go inside and help herself. "And bring one out for Cheryl." Then he added, after a moment, "And you might as well bring me out another beer."

Heather did those things and by the time she got back Cheryl had finished that particular sketch and was ready to sit down for a while.

So the three of them sat there in the warm afternoon sun and talked and drank Cokes or beer and smoked cigars. Except for Cheryl and Heather, who didn't smoke.

It made a nice scene, the three of them sitting there and talking, Solomon sprawled at their feet. But it would not have made it as a *Saturday Evening Post* cover. There was a certain sentimental and appealing quality to it, but it didn't tell a story.

Every Norman Rockwell painting tells a story.

Later, after Heather had gone back to practicing her pivot shots, Olney and Cheryl put their heads together to work on their cartoons. She had some sketches she had made last week of her grandmother, who lived up in Pittsfield, leaning back in a reclining chair in her back-yard, a sun cap shielding her eyes, and wearing dark glasses. Resting. In the same frame was Olney sitting in a chair to her right, looking at her, a cigar and a can of beer on the table beside him, saying funny things.

Four panels. Like in newspaper comic strips.

Now all they needed was for Olney to think of funny things to say.

This was going to be the hard part.

"Think of something funny to say."

Olney said he was trying.

He said, "I'm a retired plumber, remember. Not a standup comedian who had to quit because his legs gave out on him."

That was sort of funny. But not something they could use.

Brenda Sohmner, one of Olney's three tenants, pulled into the driveway.

Brenda was five feet six, blond, heavy, with open cheer-fulness and good humor. She talked a lot and liked to laugh. Forty years old. She lived in Westport, Connecti-cut, made a living writing magazine articles and stories and was in Stockbridge this summer doing research and working on a novel. She planned to return to Westport in October.

When she took the apartment she confided to Olney that she was working on a novel that would be a best seller and would shake the people of Stockbridge to their roots. She had not explained just why or how it would do that, but she had seemed confident that it would.

She said hello to Cheryl, waved to Heather, turned down Olney's offer of a beer. She said she had spent the afternoon in town talking with an old lady who knew everything about everyone in Stockbridge and she wanted to get upstairs and type up her notes while they were still fresh in her mind.

But she took time to ask Olney how his day had been.

He said it had been a good day.

"Some evening when I'm not working I'll come down and sit with you and tell you some things about Stockbridge and your tenants that you'll find interesting."

"All right."

"You have a more interesting combination of tenants than you realize."

He took a sip of his beer.

"I'll try to get down tomorrow night after dinner."

He nodded a time or two to indicate that he'd probably be here.

He'd be here because this was where he was most evenings, and not because he had any interest in hearing about things that didn't concern him, such as other people's private lives.

Later, after the girls had gone home, Olney sat by himself for a while. Watched the changing shapes of the shadows on the slopes of the Berkshire Hills, listened to the music of the Children's Chimes from the village green on West Main Street.

He heard, "The Bells of Saint Mary's," "Red River Valley," and "In Your Sweet Little Alice Blue Gown."

All good songs.

Neither of Olney's children had been back to Stockbridge since their mother's funeral, but they kept in touch by telephone. They were concerned about him, as he was about them.

That's not the worst relationship a father can have with his children.

He got a call from his daughter that night. And the conversation went about as usual.

"How are you doing?"

"Fine. How about you?"

"Great. Keeping busy." And she listed some of the things she was busy doing.

"How's Tom and the kids?"

She said they were fine. And asked how he was feeling.

He covered that subject to her satisfaction. Not eating or drinking or smoking too much. Getting exercise.

"Didn't run two miles today, though."

A moment or two, then she asked if he usually ran two miles a day and he said no. "Didn't do it today, either."

All right.

She said she was glad he hadn't lost his sense of humor. Then asked how he and his tenants were getting along. And asked what they were like. He told her that one was a woman writer who was writing a novel that would shake the people of Stockbridge to their roots, one was a teacher who used to be a college basketball player, and one was a very attractive young woman who was about to get engaged to a young man with a lot of money.

"Are you getting out more?"

He admitted that he wasn't getting out a lot, but he had two good friends who came up to visit him almost every day.

She was glad to hear that. She had been afraid that after having been married to one woman for over forty years, he might have trouble getting back into the social scene.

He said it had been easier than he had expected.

"You may even want to get married again."

Olney said, "That's possible. Maybe getting married again would be a good idea."

(His son, John, took a different approach. John thought Olney should sell the building and go down to Florida and buy one of those charter fishing boats and take people out on fishing trips and parties. Or maybe even start his own plumbing business again. Keep himself busy and his mind occupied. Retiring too early is a dangerous thing to do.)

Olney said maybe he should talk to Tom and the kids. "These long-distance phone calls must cost you a fortune."

Tom and the grandchildren got on the phone and they all took turns asking when he was coming out for another visit, and he said he would one of these days. Soon. Maybe this fall.

Everyone was having fun and they all agreed that there was no better place in the world than California.

After a while they hung up and Olney got back to the TV in time to see the Red Sox lose to the Yankees in the tenth inning on a home run by Winfield.

Two

It had never been Olney's intention to spend the last years of his life sitting on a patio during the summer and watching television in his room during the winter. But sometimes things happen that wrench a person's life away from its planned course and you can only sit stunned and immobile in one spot for a while and try to pull things together.

He had finally started doing that. Getting himself together. But, as he had told Solomon, it is not an easy thing to do. And takes a while.

The reason he had discussed the matter with Solomon was because the dog had gone through a similar experience a few months ago. His owner, a young man in his early twenties, had been killed in an automobile accident late one night. The young man's woman friend, a waitress at the Red Lion Inn, mentioned to Olney one night when he was having dinner, that the dog had become depressed and she needed to find a good home for him. Did he know anyone who would like to have a good dog? She said she wasn't home enough to give the dog the care he needed.

Olney didn't hesitate. He said he'd take the dog, of course. You don't turn down the chance to help a woman in trouble. Everyone knows that.

She described the dog as not really good looking, but friendly and faithful.

You can't ask for much more than that.

Olney drove to her house the next morning, got the dog, brought him home, unresisting and uncomplaining. But not happy. The dog turned down Olney's offer of food and water on the deck and didn't give much attention to what Olney said about the death of a loved one being something he himself had had to deal with not long ago.

"It'll get easier to accept after some time has passed," Olney said. "So take your time. Don't try to rush it."

The dog stood there looking at him for a moment or two, then turned and walked slowly down the driveway, stopped briefly at the curb, then crossed the street and lay down on the grass with his head between his paws and looked out toward the hills.

Olney went inside and got himself a beer and a cigar and sat and waited. Every once in a while he'd look down at the dog and the dog would look up at him. Then about the time he'd finished the can of beer, the dog got up and came slowly up the driveway, sprawled on the deck a few feet away and fell asleep.

"You're a good dog," Olney said. "That was a wise decision."

He named the dog Solomon.

What he and his wife had planned was that this would be their base of operations, as well as a source of income. A permanent address. A place to come home to after a trip somewhere. Fresh sheets for the bed, kindling for a quick fire in the fireplace, and something in the liquor cabinet for a welcome-home toast to themselves.

Olney had worked all his life. So had she. Neither had gone beyond high school. After Olney bought the business from the man he had worked for, she had been the book-keeper and person in charge when he was out. No long vacations or big expenses. The game plan was for early retirement and long leisurely trips across the great wide USA. Seeing all the parts of it that they had always thought they'd like to see. Trips to see their children and grandchildren. A month or two in Florida during the winter, maybe. Someplace on the water, where the fishing was good.

Maybe a trip or two to Europe or somewhere.

Due to hard work and some good luck, money wouldn't be a problem. Olney had bought the building where his store was located and the building next to it. Neither cost a lot of money at the time. But by the time they left Northampton property values had skyrocketed.

Neither of Olney's parents was alive. His mother had died the summer after he graduated from high school. His father had died in the summer of 1942. Six months after Pearl Harbor. Olney got a three day pass to get home for the funeral. Two weeks later he was on a troopship heading east across the Atlantic, and ten days after that his wife gave birth to a baby girl.

So be it.

Old people die, children are born, and young men go off to war.

Olney and Cheryl were working on their cartoons and Heather was praticing her jump shots.

Otis's car pulled into the driveway, and Olney moved his arm enough to make a slight gesture of greeting. A moment later he mumbled something about not being able to move, but that there was beer in the refrigerator if Otis wanted one.

Otis was the tenant who was the school teacher. He was twenty-eight years old, wore dark-rimmed glasses, was very tall and slender, and had dark hair that looked as if it hadn't been combed for several days. His face was thin and his Adam's apple a bit too prominent. He had played basketball in high school and college and as he approached it was clear that he was watching Heather's efforts with a critical eye.

He said, "In a minute, Olney. Let me talk to Heather first."

He walked over to where she was retrieving the ball, asked for it, and reminded her for the hundredth time to keep her elbow in. And to follow through more.

He moved back a few feet, pivoted, jumped, and sent the ball through the net. Got the ball, moved back even farther, did the same thing. Retrieved the ball, handed it to Heather. He watched her take a shot or two, gave his approval, went back to where Olney was.

"I got some papers to grade, Olney. I'd better do that and get it over with."

He said he'd try to get down for a while a little later.

A few minutes later, DeeDee Mason, Olney's third tenant, showed up.

She, too, didn't have time for a beer. She had to get dressed because Charles was taking her to the country club for dinner.

DeeDee was only eighteen years old. She was five feet eight, strawberry blond, with a perfect figure, and a sort of shy, bashful little smile that went well with everything else. Most people would agree that she was probably the most beautiful young woman in Berkshire County. Maybe even in the whole state of Massachusetts.

She had left home because her mother didn't approve of the man she was going out with and planned to marry. The man's name was Charles DeWitt, the only son of Derek and the late Linda DeWitt, one of Stockbridge's oldest and most prominent families, and wealthiest. He was a senior partner in the DeWitt-Langston Investment Services in Pittsfield. Tall, blond, athletic, and good looking. Why her mother objected to him was something DeeDee found impossible to understand.

Charles was thirty years old. But her mother didn't seem to object to the fact that he was so much older than DeeDee. In her mother's family the women tended to marry older men.

Charles had got her a part-time job as typist in his company. Nothing wrong with that. One would also assume that he had got her the car she drove to and from work. And no doubt had provided the money for the first month's rent.

Sometimes she stayed out all night. Which was all right, as far as Olney was concerned. Had she been his daughter, it wouldn't have been all right. But she wasn't his daughter.

Olney believed that everyone should be allowed to live their life the way they wanted to as long as they weren't hurting others. Olney lived his life the way he wanted to and anyone who didn't like it could go to hell.

Cheryl and Olney finished their first cartoon.

Not great, but not bad. A beginning, anyway.

It showed an older woman, modeled by Cheryl's grandmother in Pittsfield, leaning back in a reclining chair outdoors. Dark glasses and a sun cap shading her face. Olney sat in a chair to her right, holding a can of beer and talking to her. On the table next to him was an ashtray with a cigar in it and a bit of smoke curling up.

Four panels.

Olney had all the lines.

"Berkshire Savings called today."

"They said you were a little short at the bank."

"I said you were a little short at home too."

"But I liked you that way."

Olney said he'd got the idea from the fact that he found this morning he'd made an error in his checkbook, and that Cheryl had said once that her grandmother was short of money.

Anyway, Olney suggested they celebrate by walking into town for ice cream cones.

"I want to see if Heather wants to come."

Olney said, "Of course. And Solomon can come along, too. If he wants to."

So they did. The four of them. Heather with her basketball and Cheryl with her sketch pad. And on their way a couple of nice middle-aged ladies who'd just come from the Norman Rockwell Museum saw them and took their picture.

Later that evening, Olney and Solomon alone on the patio, Brenda came down with a drink and a book and said she wanted to show Olney something.

He turned down the radio, out of politeness, and knowing that the Red Sox would probably lose anyway. She pulled a chair close to him and opened the book.

The book was a collection of paintings by Norman Rockwell. One of which was apparently of particular interest.

Olney took a sip of beer, lit a fresh cigar, and gave it his partly undivided attention.

She explained it to him.

The painting was called *The Honeymooners* and showed three young boys sitting on the low stone wall in front of the Stockbridge library. It is summer. The day is hot. The kids have just finished a game of baseball and look tired but happy. You get the feeling that their team won.

Each boy has one or more parts of a baseball uniform. Maybe shirt or trousers, spiked shoes, baseball cap. None has a complete outfit. One is holding a baseball bat, another holds a bat and ball, and two old ballgloves lie at their feet. Both bats have been repaired with adhesive tape and the baseball is coming apart at the seams, with short bits of string popping out. A small black and white dog of no particular breed sits at their feet. The dog has a small dirty bandage on one paw.

The three boys are watching, with mixed expressions, two young honeymooners walking by.

The focus is on the star of the picture, the blushing young bride, her hair done up in pigtails, looking shy, frail, and very embarrassed. She grips the arm of her new husband as if he were all that kept her from sinking down out of sight forever.

The groom is a good looking young man with a strong profile, looking straight ahead. He is oblivious to the kids sitting on the wall. His face shows confidence, pride, and the determination to protect forever the lovely young woman he has taken as his bride. He is wearing a suit that doesn't quite fit. You would guess that the suit was bought in a country store or from a travelling salesman.

In the background is a middle-aged waitress, a package and some letters under her arm, presumably on her way from the post office back to her job at the Red Lion Inn. On her face is the sentimental expression of one who is recalling the time years ago when she, too, was a happy and blushing bride. It is a nice expression. She is happy for them. She wishes them well.

Brenda said that the reason this particular painting would interest Olney was that the model for the blushing young bride was DeeDee's mother, Rhonda.

Olney heard the announcer say that Jim Rice had grounded out, ending the inning.

Brenda said that the model for the groom was a young man named Tacy Van Rensselaer. He was twenty-one and she was eighteen.

That had been twenty years ago.

She pointed in turn to each of the three boys on the low wall.

"That's Charles DeWitt. The man DeeDee is going to marry."

She pointed to another. "And that's our Otis. Otis Markham."

To the third boy. "And that's a local boy named Billie Cooter."

Charles had been ten, Billie nine, and Otis, already tall for his age, eight.

The model for the waitress was a woman from Pittsfield named Mary Ostrowski. She was the only one in the painting Brenda didn't know.

After the painting was finished and had become a cover on the *Saturday Evening Post,* Derek DeWitt, Charles's father, had given a big party at his estate for Rockwell and the models. Steaks on the grill, champagne, soft drinks for the kids. And swimming in the pool for anyone who wished to do so.

Norman Rockwell was there with his wife. Rockwell's photographer and his family were there. The only person who didn't attend was the woman who had modeled for the waitress.

Before the party ended, Rockwell did something really nice.

Norman Rockwell gave Rhonda the painting. Not a print or photograph, but the original painting.

"He often did that," Brenda said. "He was a sentimental and generous person."

No one realized at the time what a valuable gift Rhonda had received. "That painting," Brenda said, "today would probably be worth at least a hundred thousand dollars. Maybe much more than that."

Brenda said that in a couple of months there was going to be a big reunion for all those who had modeled for the painting. August twenty-second, to be exact. This time on the estate of Tacy Van Rensselaer, now forty-one years old, with three fine children and a lovely wife, and about to start his campaign for state senator. He had recently bought the original painting, which Rhonda had had to sell many years ago, and would have it on display at the party. He was also having a replica of the low stone wall built so everyone could pose just as they had done for the original painting.

"So if you hear people talking about Tacy's party and a painting called *The Honeymooners,* you'll know what they are talking about."

All right. Olney nodded. He turned the radio up a little.

She wasn't finished. She wanted to tell him about what had happened to the people in the painting.

He turned the radio back down a little.

The worst to one of the boys seated on the low wall. Billie Cooter. He had not returned alive from VietNam.

He said, "You can skip Otis and Charles. I already know about them."

She chose not to. She said, "Charles grew up to become a successful investment counselor. And is about to become engaged to DeeDee. Otis went to college on an athletic scholarship, then to graduate school, and now teaches at Berkshire Community College."

"And lives here in this apartment," Olney said, "and lectures Heather for not keeping her elbow in."

Brenda said, "Right. That's our Otis."

Tacy, the young groom, graduated from law school, then came back to Stockbridge and joined his father's law firm. He married a woman from one of the old Stockbridge families, dabbled in politics, was now taking the big plunge. Candidate for state senator.

Rhonda Mason, now the mother of four, had found it difficult to handle all the flattering things people said about how beautiful she was. Derek DeWitt, Charles's father, even told her that probably she could become a model in New York City if she wanted to. And if she wanted to try, he'd be willing to help her.

Even then, twenty years ago, Derek DeWitt had more money than he knew what to do with. In addition to the money he had inherited, he had a very lucrative practice as a psychiatrist in Manhattan. He came back to Stockbridge weekends. Most weekends, anyway. In New York he had a penthouse on the east side, entertained lavishly, had friends in advertising, theater, and television.

He told Rhonda he knew a lot of people who would love to take a chance on an attractive new face. Especially a face as attractive as hers.

So she tried it. Went to New York, and Derek had helped all he could. Helped her buy the right clothes and be seen in the right places. But it hadn't turned out well. It is not easy for a naive young woman from a small town in New England to break into the modeling profession in the big city.

"The end," Brenda said, "came when she got pregnant by a man who wouldn't marry her."

Then Brenda looked at Olney and asked, "Do you want to know the rest of the story? It's not too happy."

He said that he didn't.

She told him anyway.

Derek kept helping her. He bought her painting from her so she would have money enough to get back to Stockbridge.

"Remember," Brenda said, "we are talking about the Derek DeWitt who is the father of the man DeeDee is going to marry."

Olney said he thought he had that part of it straight.

"Rhonda came back, two months pregnant. Married Henry Mason, an older man over in Lee, had the baby, DeeDee, then three more kids. A boy and two girls."

She said, "One day Henry Mason simply left for parts unknown and hasn't been heard from since. Rhonda worked at the supermarket in Lee to support the family. Then a few years ago the company went out of business and she couldn't find another job. And now the woman who once modeled as the blushing young bride in one of Norman Rockwell's greatest paintings is today on public welfare."

Olney felt bad about that. He took another look at the young strawberry blond in the painting, saw the same kind of small shy smile that DeeDee had now.

"How come you are so involved in all this?"

"I'm involved," Brenda said. "Very much involved. Believe me."

She wasn't finished. There was more.

She explained that Rockwell first photographed his models in his studio, then painted from the photographs. He had a room with an assortment of props, and when a model came to the studio to be photographed, the prop room usually provided something helpful. The middle-aged waitress in the background, she pointed out, was wearing a waitress uniform from the prop room.

After Rockwell died, Tacy bought some items from the famous prop room. So, at the twenty-year reunion, when the photographers take pictures of the re-enactment, the baseball bats and gloves and the baseball coming apart at the seams will be the same ones Rockwell used in the original painting.

She thought that would be a nice touch. Rockwell would have loved it.

All right.

He turned the radio back up a little.

"This painting," Brenda said, "deeply affected all the people who were in it." And took a moment for that to sink in.

"For two of them it's likely to end in tragedy."

Olney said, "I hope not." Then turned up the radio a bit more. Someone had hit a home run, apparently.

He said, "Brenda, I don't involve myself in other people's private lives. Unless I'm asked to. If those two people, whoever they are, feel I can help them in any way all they have to do is ask. Otherwise I'll keep out of it."

"They won't ask."

"Then there's nothing I can do."

After things quieted down a bit, the announcer gave the score. It was the Yankees six to two.

Olney said, "Those damn Red Sox."

He said, "Sometimes, I wish I'd been born in Texas so I could root for the Houston Astros."

She said, "Someday maybe I'll tell you, anyway."

She went back upstairs to work on her novel and Olney sat and watched the sun getting ready to call it a day. Spent a few moments wishing his wife were still alive. Probably the only woman he'd ever known he could stand being around for very long.

"Want to take a walk?"

Walk was a word Solomon knew. He stood up and wagged his tail.

"How about Bowker Woods?"

That was all right with Solomon.

They got into the car and drove over to Route 183 past Mundy's and into Bowker Woods and parked. Walked past the pond with the carp and goldfish and bullfrogs and down the path that wound between the trees. Mostly pine and birch and maple. Then into a large open meadow with tall grass and nothing else.

Solomon disappeared into the high grass, reappearing every once in a while. Leaping up, rushing at something or other, stopping to investigate something else. Into the woods, then out again.

It must make a dog feel good to get away from the house and out to where he understands what's going on. Away from things that make no sense, like someone bouncing a round object up and down on the cement and throwing it for no good reason at something up over the garage doors. People jumping up and down and chasing one another around.

Things like that.

Solomon came out of the woods temporarily, looked over to make sure Olney was still there, turned and ran back into the woods and barked some more.

Ordinarily, when they came here, Olney circled the meadow counterclockwise along the edge of the woods. This time, for some reason, he didn't do that. He walked out into the middle of the open space and just stood there. It gave him a strange feeling. Something about standing there so open and exposed and alone. A solitary human being. Unarmed. Unprotected. Nothing there to hide behind or dive into.

He wondered what a person would think seeing an old man just standing out there in the middle of the meadow. Alone.

He put his hands in his pockets, slowly turned around every once in a while. Nothing happened. No animal attacked him. No human being yelled at him. Or shot at him. Or came running happily with a bouquet of flowers and a can of cold beer.

He remembered times when it wasn't safe to raise your head more than an inch above the level of the foxhole. And he wondered what had ever happened to Sergeant Blandon. If Olney had ever got up and walked out into the middle of a field and just stood there like this, Blandon would have shot him himself as an example to the others. Not just for standing up, but for going out alone.

But the war is over. Life itself is mostly over. He thought back to years ago when he had walked through

fields like this with his father and brothers, carrying shot-
guns, waiting for one of the dogs to flush a covey of quail
or a pheasant. But had a covey of quail now suddenly
exploded into the air with a fury of feathers, Olney would
only have apologized for disturbing them.

He gave a long whistle, and a moment later Solomon
came out of the woods. Together they headed back to the
car.

When they made the left turn on Glendale Road they
faced head-on a nearly full golden moon rising just above
the tree tops. Olney pulled off to one side of the road for a
minute or two so they could enjoy the sight of it.

The feeling of standing alone in the middle of that field
stayed with him. A man shouldn't go out alone. Not
because it isn't safe, but because it isn't fun. Before long he
was going to have to figure out what to do about his
problem of being alone so much.

Three

Mary Ostrowski, sixty-three years old, sort of short, slender, medium-length dark gray hair with a few lines of black running through it, was, in her own way, attractive. She had grayish blue eyes, a soft expression, and a way of holding her chin up ever so slightly that gave her an alert, almost birdlike look. She lived in a quiet residential neighborhood just off South Street in Pittsfield, Massachusetts, in a large white house with green shutters and a tall hedge across the front of the property. She and Paul had bought it shortly after they were married. Big enough for the family they planned to have, close enough to the Pittsfield School of Music, where Paul taught, and within walking distance of the Pittsfield library where Mary worked.

That was a long time ago.

Mary Ostrowski lived by herself now, so the house was much too large and the high hedge in front and along the side made the property seem too isolated. A person could sit in the side yard out of sight of everyone and feel too much alone.

There were two large maple trees, one in front and one in the middle of the side yard, both of which she and Paul had planted shortly after moving in. There were lilac bushes and a flower garden in the back. There was also a faded and worn orange striped hammock. And a small and rather cluttered screened-in side porch.

Mary often felt that she should either take in boarders or sell the house and buy something smaller. But she didn't really want to move. And although taking in boarders would provide a welcome extra income, it would also mean losing the delightful privacy of her side yard and life.

She had a friend, Florence, a retired school teacher who lived across the street and came over frequently to sit in Mary's yard because she had no yard of her own. She was not the most exciting company in the world, but better than no company at all. And it wouldn't be nice to turn away someone who enjoys sitting in a side yard and doesn't have one of her own.

Mary Ostrowski, almost two years a widow, lived what she considered a good life. Not a very active social life anymore, but still there were occasional concerts, plays, or movies. She read the *New York Times* and kept up with the current literary world. She knew the children of the neighborhood, and sometimes on their way home from school they would come up the sidewalk and say hello. And maybe sit down and talk awhile. And she might mention that there was some candy in that little basket on the kitchen table and they could help themselves if they'd like. Which they usually did.

Sometimes she felt that maybe she was getting just a little bit too comfortable with the image of herself as a nice little old lady having tea in the side yard and candy in the kitchen for children. She had lately begun using the hammock more, although it was a little tricky getting into or out of it. And more frequently a glass or two of wine instead of tea all the time.

Like many best made plans, the ones she and Paul had made had gone awry. She had quit her job at the library two years ago because Paul was about to retire from his job at the music school. They had figured out that with his retirement income and their combined social security they would be able to afford to travel, on a limited budget, of course, and have time to pursue the many things they were interested in. Musical composition by him, including maybe a symphony. Serious writing for her. Maybe a book of poems or short stories. Maybe even a novel.

Then, only a few weeks after she had left the library, the month before Paul was to retire, a longtime friend of theirs, Charlie Griffith, had one morning come slowly and reluctantly up the front walk. Mary had happened to see him coming. Had gone out to meet him.

It had to be something out of the ordinary that would bring Charlie up the walk this time of day.

Charlie worked with Paul at the school. He was a tall, thin, somewhat doleful looking man. Honest, straightforward, and intelligent. He and his wife were probably Paul's and her best friends. A friendship going back at least two decades. Nearly three.

He said, "I have bad news, Mary." And the unhappy look on his face confirmed the truth of that.

"What is it?"

He said, "Paul had a heart attack."

She felt she almost didn't have to ask. But she did, anyway.

"Is he dead?"

"Yes, Mary."

Then he held her while she cried. And cried himself.

Mary had three children. All different.

Pauline, her oldest, thirty-six, divorced, independent, and resembling more and more, as Mary often noticed, the businessman husband she had found it so impossible to live with. She was bright, attractive, and athletic. She had some kind of junior executive position with Beltics Corporation in Lee. She sometimes took Mary to lunch at the Colonial Hilton on her expense account.

Mary's son, Gregory, thirty-three, was a talented musician making the kind of music she and Paul had found intolerable. Hard music that was electronic, amplified, and ear splitting. Mindless. She would have told him that, had it not been that he was her son and she loved him.

Her youngest, Rosemary, had been the hippie flower child. Had dropped out of college early, got married, then pregnant. Or vice versa. Then travelled across the country strewing flowers or holding up a protest sign, lived in communes or wherever, but throughout it all had borne and cared for a delightful and talented little girl now ten years old. Named Cheryl.

Rosemary, thirty years old, divorced, was a waitress in Stockbridge and attended evening classes at Berkshire Community College.

Mary accepted philosophically the differences between her children's life styles and her own. Young people have the right to live life their own way. She remembered Gregory saying something once about doing whatever turns you on.

All right.

Mary Ostrowski picked up a little extra money giving piano lessons to children. One of her pupils was a seven-year-old who lived in Lenox. Mary went there Saturday mornings. On the way home she usually stopped in the Lenox bookstore to exchange pleasantries and maybe buy a book or two.

It was there, one Saturday morning, that Mary found the book that changed her life. She found it downstairs among the used books. It was written by a Dr. J.T. Whorter, was marked down to only a dollar and ninety-five cents, and was called *Don't Grow Old Alone Unless You Want To*.

It was a slim volume, with line drawings, and was apparently intended for an older audience. She couldn't decide at first if it was intended to be serious, funny, or both. She happened to open it to a page in a chapter dealing with the problems of older couples spending their first night in bed together, and here Dr. Whorter was suggesting that in order not to break the romantic spell, he or she might consider for that one night maybe not putting their partial plate in a glass of water on the table by the bed.

On future nights, of course, it would be all right.

To show how it would be on future nights, there was a line drawing of two glasses of water, side by side, each with a partial plate in it. Marked, of course, *His* and *Hers*.

All right.

Maybe the book would be good for a few laughs, if nothing more.

When she paid for the book, she saw that the woman behind the desk looked at it and smiled.

Mary asked, "Is this a book of psychology or humor?"

The lady said she didn't know. She had glanced through it when it first came in, trying to decide which shelf to put it on. She finally had decided that it was a sort of tongue in cheek self-help book for people middle-aged and older. She said she thought it might be fun to read, but probably shouldn't be taken seriously.

"He admits that he makes up his own statistics."

All right. No problem. At least he's honest.

The lady said, "After you've finished reading it, come in sometime and let me know what you thought of it."

Mary said she'd do that.

Florence, Mary's neighbor from across the street, was sitting in the side yard when Mary got home.

Florence said, "You have some messages. I put them on the dining room table."

Mary didn't want messages put on her dining room table.

"I wish you wouldn't do that, Florence. Please don't answer the phone for me when I'm away."

Florence said, "The phone kept ringing. I can't just sit out here and let the phone ring."

Mary said, "Pretend it's coming from next door."

But that sounded a bit harsh, so Mary laughed and said, 'It's all right this time, Florence. But I wish you wouldn't do it."

She went inside, found the messages, set them aside and went into the kitchen. She made herself a cup of tea, took it into the living room, settled into a comfortable chair by the window and spent a while skimming through Dr. Whorter's book. After ten or fifteen minutes she still couldn't decide if it was supposed to be simply entertaining or actually good and useful advice.

Dr. Whorter said that 80% of those widows who do remarry start making plans one and three-quarter years after the death of their spouse. For men it is a year and a half.

That was interesting.

Mary had been a widow for one year and eight months. Within the last few weeks she had felt something stirring inside her that she couldn't quite identify. A restlessness. A certain dissatisfaction. A muted longing.

The she remembered that it was spring. Which explained everything. Even older women are affected by that time of the year when the flowers are blooming and the days are warm.

Dr. Whorter said that only two percent of the women who are widowed and living alone at age sixty-two ever marry again.

Even though you knew he was making up his own statistics, when you're sixty-three years old, that's scary.

She got up and went to the door to let the cats in.

She said, "C'mon in, kids."

The kids were Melanie and Sandy. Beautiful and long-haired and affectionate.

"I was wondering where you were."

Dr. Whorter had something to say about that.

He said that eighty-three percent of older people who live alone sooner or later start talking to their pets.

He said don't worry about it.

She put the book aside and picked up the phone messages.

One was from a Tacy Van Rensselaer, whom she had never heard of. One was from her son, Gregory, and the other from Mrs. Fern, Steven's mother.

Mary called Mrs. Fern and heard what she had expected to hear. That because the weather was getting so good, Steven didn't want to take piano lessons anymore. And Mary said she understood.

"If you hear of any small children needing piano lessons for beginners," Mary said, "let me know."

Mrs. Fern said she certainly would. Then they both said some nice things about summertime, kids, music, and today's weather, and hung up.

She called Gregory. He would either want to borrow her car that evening or see if maybe she had room for a couple friends from out of town to spend the night. He had a van that he used to haul his equipment, but sometimes he'd borrow her car to lend to a friend to get other friends to wherever it was they were playing. And sometimes he had musicians sitting in with his group who were from out of town and could use a place to stay so they wouldn't have to drive a long way home late at night.

It was the car. She said she planned to use it that evening but how was he doing and how was last night at the Hillside House in Dalton.

He said that the crowd loved them. They had played until closing time, but still they wanted more. It had been almost impossible to get them to leave.

"Sounds good."

Gregory played lead guitar in a group he had put together himself. This group was doing better than the ones he had started earlier, but not so much so that offers were coming in from all over the country. Not even from all over the county. But contemporary music, she had been told, is a highly competitive business and to survive in it at all is a sign of success.

She took his word for it.

Before she hung up, she relented and said he could use her car if he really needed it.

Mary called the Van Rensselaer number and a woman answered.

"I'm Mary Ostrowski. Someone named Tacy Van Rensselaer left a message for me to call him."

The woman said he was out at the moment. He would be back in about an hour.

"Could you tell me who he is and what he wants?" She said, "I don't want to buy anything."

The woman seemed a bit offended at that. She said, "Mr. Van Rensselaer is Attorney Van Rensselaer. I assure you he is not trying to sell you anything."

"Whatever it is," Mary said, "I'm innocent. I didn't do it." And she added, "Tell me what it is he wants."

"I'd prefer he told you."

"I'd prefer you told me."

For a moment, nothing. Then the woman said, "You modeled for a painting by Norman Rockwell twenty years ago. It was called *The Honeymooners*. Mr. Van Rensselaer recently acquired the painting. He plans a big reunion party for the people who modeled for the painting.

She said, "But I want him to tell you about it."

"Are you his wife?"

She said she was.

"Mrs. Van Rensselaer, I recall the painting. That was a long time ago. I appreciate your husband inviting me, but

I really am not interested in attending a reunion party of those who were in the painting."

"I'll have him call you."

"He would be wasting his time. Please just tell him I said I really don't want to attend. But thanks."

"It will be a good party."

"I'm sure."

"He'll call you."

All right. Why argue.

They both said good-bye and hung up.

One Saturday morning, twenty years ago, Mary had been standing in front of the Stockbridge post office, waiting for someone. And smiling at the nice amusing scene of a good looking young man patting a dog on one end of a leash and trying to make the acquaintance of the attractive young woman at the other end. The dog was friendly and doing all it could to help. The young man was making progress and it obviously was only a matter of minutes before the young people exchanged names, current places of employment, where in town they were staying, and started down the street together.

Ah! Young love. How good it is.

Enough to make a sentimental forty-three-old woman smile.

A tall, thin, gray-haired man came up and introduced himself as Norman Rockwell. And asked if she would pose for him for a painting. It seemed terribly important to him that he capture just that expression that he had seen on her face moments ago. Before she had time to think about it, he had made an appointment for her to be in his studio for photographs. And was gone.

She and Paul had been visiting friends in Stockbridge for the day, with plans for Tanglewood and the Boston Symphony that night. The appointment was for next

week. They convinced her she should keep it. It would be
fun. And, in a way, an honor. After all, Norman Rockwell
was probably the country's most famous illustrator.

She kept the appointment, posed for him, first putting
on, as he asked her to do, the uniform of a waitress. He
gave her a package and an armful of mail to hold, and
asked her to look in a certain direction and try to recap-
ture the look he seen on her face that morning outside the
post office.

He had her take off her own glasses and replace them
with a larger pair with thicker lenses.

It took a while. He was patient. So was she. The
photographer took many pictures from different angles.
Finally Rockwell was satisfied. Mary got out of the waitress uniform and back into the attractive summer dress
she had been wearing. And got her own glasses back.

About three months later she saw a copy of The *Saturday
Evening Post* with a painting on the cover called *The Honeymooners*. In the background was a middle-aged woman, no
longer especially attractive, but whose face showed that
years ago she might have been. A woman who looked as if
she had herself no doubt once known love and romance,
who now could look upon a young bride and groom just
starting out in life, and could remember that she had once
been that age. And in love. And wished them well. Her
own life, you would guess, had not been a great success.
But they were a nice young couple and she was happy for
them.

At first, Mary didn't recognize herself. Rockwell had
made her look heavier, less intelligent, sentimental, and
almost foolish. All he had left her with was that one thing
he wanted: the nice, warm, kindly, friendly, sweet smile.

The man, she admitted grudgingly, had talent.

She was reading Dr. Whorter's book when Tacy Van
Rensselaer called.

She repeated what she had told his wife. That she wasn't interested.

He explained in his cheerful and persuasive voice why he was having a party, and his pride in bringing the painting back to Stockbridge where it belonged. Told of his giving it on loan to the Norman Rockwell Museum. It was, he said, undoubtedly Norman Rockwell's greatest painting.

He told her that at the reunion he would announce his candidacy for state senator. And he talked of all the people who would be there. Many from as far away as Boston.

She wasn't interested. She told him that.

He asked her to think about it, and repeated what his wife had said earlier. "It will be a good party."

Mary knew some people in Boston, good friends, but none who would likely come to the Berkshires for a political rally. She didn't even know anyone in the Berkshires of the kind who'd go to a political rally.

"Sorry, but I'm really not interested."

He asked her to think about it, said he'd call her again in a few weeks to see if she had changed her mind.

She said she wouldn't. She was sure of that.

She was wrong. According to Dr. Whorter. She realized that a few minutes later when she got a little further into Dr. Whorter's book.

One of the things Dr. Whorter advised older women was this:

Never turn down an invitation to a large party simply because you won't know anyone. Quite the contrary. If someone invites you to a small party and tells you that you will enjoy yourself because you will know everyone there, you might as well stay home. You already know them. You've probably worked with most of them in the same office for twenty years. On the other hand, it is at the big parties where you don't know anyone that you are most likely to meet just that person you've been looking for but couldn't find. The more new people you meet, he pointed out, the greater the chance that you might find that certain kind of man who is just what you are looking for.

Mary was well aware of the kind of man she was looking for. He would be intelligent, cultivated, good looking. Enjoyed literature and good music. Loved European travel. Successful in one of the arts.

Mary got up and got herself a glass of wine. Then back to the chair and book.

She said, "Kids, we got to do something."

One thing Dr. Whorter suggested was that at least once a day you say out loud: "I do not want to grow old all by myself."

She tried that.

"I do not want to grow old all by myself."

Sandy slept on. But Melanie got up and came over and rubbed up against her leg.

Four

The way Cheryl held her pencil when she sketched reminded Olney of a girl in the fourth grade who made a fist like that when she wrote. A rounded chubby fist. He didn't recall her name, but he remembered that she was short, blond, good humored, and very bright. He wondered what ever happened to her. Something good, he hoped.

Cheryl asked, "What are you smiling about?"

He said he just happened to be remembering something.

"What?"

"Some girl about your age I knew back in the fourth grade."

"Were you in love with her?"

"I don't think so. Back in those days you didn't fall in love when you were only nine or ten years old." He said, "Usually not until you were eleven."

She said she wasn't ever going to fall in love. All she wanted to do was be an artist.

He said that artists fall in love same as other people.

"Heather isn't going to fall in love either." Then she asked if he had ever been in love and he told her yes. He said he recommended it for everyone.

They were on the patio working on their cartoons. That was the morning he got the call from DeeDee's mother, Rhonda Mason.

They had just finished their fourth cartoon. This one from an idea Olney got from reading a magazine advertisement about a drink that makes you feel so happy that you're sure you're in love. In this one, Olney was holding a magazine instead of a can of beer. The beer was on the table with the cigar and ashtray.

Just as in the first three, Olney was speaking to the woman semi-napping in her reclining chair at his left. This time she had a few words.

"The man was working nights in the lab on a secret formula."
"One sip and you think you're in love."
"Did he find it?"
"They'll never know."
"He ran off with the cleaning lady."

Sometimes Cheryl wasn't sure if Olney's lines were funny or not. Which was all right. They had agreed at the beginning that she did the drawing and he did the jokes.

He said that in this case the joke was that the man had found the secret formula just as the cleaning lady started mopping the floor.

The reason Rhonda called was that she wanted to invite him to lunch.

Rhonda said that DeeDee had told her so much about him that she felt she just had to meet him.

"Can you come to lunch tomorrow?"

Olney said he'd love to, because he had heard so much about her, too, but he'd already promised an old friend in Northampton that he'd drive over there and take him fishing tomorrow. The man was getting old and really looked forward to these fishing trips. Olney wouldn't dare disappoint the old man.

She understood, of course.

So she suggested he come over today. There was still time. If he got there by one o'clock the children would have finished their lunch and gone out to play. She would have some sandwiches and they'd eat on the porch and talk.

This was more than a casual invitation to lunch. He could tell that. There was almost a hint of desperation in her voice.

Olney didn't want to go. But he couldn't think of a good excuse. He could have said that he had a dental appointment or something, but he didn't think of that until after he had hung up.

He returned to the patio to tell Cheryl that he had to leave in a little while because he had been invited to lunch and hadn't been able to think of an excuse for not going.

"I was never good at thinking fast on my feet."

He said, "I'm even worse sitting down."

She said, "That's not bad, Olney. You're getting funnier."

"Thanks." And they went back to work on their cartoons.

Cheryl said her grandmother thought the characters in the cartoons should have names. So the readers would get to think of them as real people.

Cheryl thought the characters should have funny names. For the man, a funny name like Horace.

Olney vetoed that.

"You can call the woman anything you want," he said, "but the man is going to have a simple ordinary name. Like Bill."

Anyway, he couldn't work on cartoons any longer today. He had to pick some tomatoes and things to take to the woman he had to have lunch with.

Then he had to go inside and change his shirt.

"When I get back I'm going to dig some worms and go fishing. If you want to go fishing you'll have to get permission from your mother. And if Heather wants to come along, she'll have to get permission from her mother, too."

"She lives with her grandmother."

"Okay, grandmother."

He said he hoped he wouldn't have to stay more than an hour.

Rhonda Mason lived five miles away in Lee, in a small brown house in an unpretentious neighborhood of working people. The paved street was a long narrow playground. Kids were skipping rope, playing hopscotch, throwing baseballs, riding bikes. Lots of shouting.

The Mason house, like most of the others, looked to be not so much run down as simply being neglected temporarily until more important matters were taken care of. Food and shoes and winter jackets. Things like that. The backyard had been worn down to bare earth. Kids were swinging on an old tire at the end of a long rope hung from a tree. There were a few bicycles leaning against the fence and scattered remains of others at the back end of the lot.

Two dogs.

All in all, not a bad scene. Kids having fun.

Rhonda Mason was about five feet six, slender, still attractive. Late thirties. Slightly faded strawberry blond, with a shy frailness that gave her a sort of virginal look. Maybe not recently virginal, but once, anyway. Blue eyes, nice smile, and the slightly worried look appropriate to a mother of four children.

You could see that she was the bride in Rockwell's painting, only twenty years later.

Olney had brought a bottle of wine, a six pack of beer, some tomatoes, summer squash, and peas from the garden. He said the beer was all he would drink, so she could save the wine, if she wished, to have with dinner some night. He apologized for the tomatoes not being quite as ripe as they could be and for the green peas being a bit past their prime.

They sat at a table on the screened-in side porch, had ham and cheese sandwiches and salad and talked children and things. He told about his married son and daughter in California and the six grandchildren. She asked if he had any pictures with him and he said he didn't. Although actually he did. In his wallet. But he wasn't as interested in talking about grandchildren as he was in getting home and going fishing.

All three of her children managed to find some reason for coming in to ask their mother about something or other. And to see who was the man their mother was having lunch with.

Her son, James, fifteen, was slender, polite, soft spoken, with a slightly troubled look about him. Millie and Melissa, twelve and nine, were shy, well mannered, strawberry blond like their mother, and very curious about Olney.

Rhonda was patient with them, got them back outside to play, and asked them nicely to play a little ways from the house so she and her friend could hear themselves talk.

She was divorced. She told him that. She said that her husband, who broke under the responsibilities of trying to support four children, drank a lot and one day simply took off for parts unknown. That had been six years ago.

Her father, a widower, was a big help. He was like a father to the kids. He worked the seven-to-three shift at the paper mill and always came by the house about three-thirty. She said she hoped Olney would be able to stay around long enough to meet him.

She did not mention that she was on public welfare. Olney knew that only because Brenda had told him.

"That would be nice," Olney said. "He sounds like a nice person. But I promised a couple kids I'd take them fishing."

He glanced at his watch. "They'll be waiting for me."

Olney took a long look at that attractive young woman with four kids and a world of problems. And ran some thoughts through his head.

Twenty years ago she was eighteen, so she was now thirty-eight. A lot of things about her were appealing. The soft face showed no signs of bitterness or anger. Her concern for the children was obvious, and he would guess that she was a warm and loving person. She would be easy to enjoy, nice to have around the house and take to bed at night.

It would be so easy to take this young woman in your arms, tell her that you loved her, that every problem she had was now yours as well, that everything was going to be all right. From now on there would be only laughter, parties, picnics, joy, and love.

But she was thirty-eight. and Olney was sixty-five.

Olney took a sip of beer and said, "Grandfathers are great for kids."

No doubt true. But that was not what she had invited him over here to talk about.

"DeeDee thinks you're the nicest person she's ever met."

He protested that, of course. And said some nice things about DeeDee.

"Another of your tenants who likes you is Brenda Sohmner."

He said some nice things about Brenda, too.

"She took me to lunch last week. Asked me a lot of questions about people around here I've known."

They had finished lunch. She lit a cigarette. Olney asked if she would mind if he smoked a cigar.

"I never smoke them in other people's houses, but I thought that out here on the porch it might be all right."

She said she didn't mind. She liked the smell of cigars. Millie and Melissa were in for drinks of water and to ask if she thought grandfather would take them to the park after he got off work. She said she knew he would if they asked him to. And now please go outside and play.

They left, and she asked Olney if he'd heard of the big party Tacy Van Rensselaer was having and had he been invited.

Ottis Markham had asked him to come as his guest, Olney said, but he'd turned down the invitation.

Olney said he'd like to open one more can of beer, then he had to go.

"He's calling it a reunion for all the models in the Rockwell painting," Rhonda said, "but what he's really doing is using us to start his campaign for state senator."

He opened the beer, and asked Rhonda if she'd like him to open one more for her.

She hesitated a moment, then said she'd changed her mind about the wine. Instead of saving it, she thought she'd open it now.

She went into the kitchen, came back with the wine and two glasses, asked Olney if he'd have some.

He said thanks, but he'd stick with the beer.

Melissa was in to say that the boys wouldn't let her play on the swing. While she talked to her mother, she looked at Olney.

Rhonda called to the boys in back to let the girls play on the swing, then ushered Melissa out the door.

While she was doing that, Olney opened the wine for her and filler her glass.

She sat down. "Children!"

He said, "I know what you mean. But they seem like great kids and I'm sure you're proud of them."

She said she was.

"They are just curious about my having a man for lunch."

She took a drink of the wine, a deep breath, and Olney sensed that she was not ready to talk about whatever it was that had caused her to invite him to lunch.

"I wish with all my heart that I had never met Norman Rockwell and never been in his painting."

A few long moments passed.

He had a sip of his beer. She a drag on her cigarette.

"DeeDee was adopted."

Olney said he knew that. He had heard DeeDee and Otis talking about it. Otis, too, had been adopted.

She took another sip. Thought for a moment.

"If that painting had not been painted, I would not have met the DeWitts, and DeeDee would never have met Charles."

Olney tried to look at his watch without seeming to do so.

What you do is you scratch a spot on the back of your hand, and as you glance down at the spot you're scratching, you look to see what time it is.

"Charles happened to see DeeDee and me together one day last winter and came right over to be introduced. Other times we met he barely bothered to say hello."

Another sip of her wine.

Then she said, "Olney, I'll tell you why I invited you here today."

Good.

She looked tired. Still rather beautiful, but tired. It showed in her eyes.

The mother of four kids, remember. You can't look eighteen forever.

"I want you to talk DeeDee out of marrying Charles."

He looked at her. Took a long sip of his beer.

"Why would you want me to do that, Rhonda?"

"Because he isn't right for her."

He crushed out his cigar.

She said, "Have you met Charles?"

Olney said he had. Once when Charles had come by to pick up DeeDee for dinner.

The ice cream wagon clanged to a halt across the street and the girls were in to ask if they could buy ice cream.

Every child knows that the time to ask your mother for ice cream money is when she has company.

Olney said, "If you don't mind, let me buy it for them. I don't get to do this very often."

She protested. But the kids didn't seem to mind.

He gave them five dollars and suggested they treat any kids who didn't have money. And if they needed more money, come back.

The screen door slammed, the kids were gone. Rhonda re-filled her glass, then continued where she had left off.

"Do you know anything about the DeWitts?"

He shook his head.

"Ask Brenda about them sometime."

Olney watched the kids around the ice cream truck.

"The DeWitts treat their women miserably. DeeDee would never be accepted in that crowd."

She had more of the wine.

"The country club. The landed-gentry crowd. The old-families circle."

He offered the comment that Charles did seem to be very fond of DeeDee.

"Only because she's beautiful," Rhonda said. "Only because he needs a wife who will live in his house and have children while he gradually gets around to spending most of his week in Manhattan and coming home weekends, if he feels like it. The way his father did."

She refilled her glass.

Olney said, "I got to go soon, Rhonda. I told the kids I'd be home by this time."

"The DeWitts go to New York, have themselves all the women they want. Young women, usually. Leave the wives in Stockbridge to care for the children and maintain the family tradition."

She said, "I'll tell you something that a lot of people don't know."

Olney scratched the back of his hand again.

"Derek DeWitt, Charles's father, had a lot of affairs with women in New York. After a while, his wife up here began having affairs, too. And told him she wanted a divorce."

Olney lit a fresh cigar.

"Brenda is going to use this in her novel. If you don't believe me, ask her."

She said, "Instead of giving her a divorce right away, he hired a detective to catch her in one of her small affairs so when she sued for divorce he'd have proof that she'd been playing around, too. And the man she was caught in bed with was a man who would have been destroyed by the scandal."

Olney couldn't think of a way to tell her that he had absolutely no interest in this. Instead, he focused his mind on how the lake was going to look in a little while. Over on the west side, where the shadows from the trees extended out over the water. The big fish came up earlier there than they did on the east side of the lake. He visualized a red bobber that one of the kids had tossed out, sitting for a moment on top of the water, starting to move just the slightest at first, then suddenly plunging down and out of sight. The line grown tight, the rod bent, and everyone yelling advice of one kind or another. Solomon barking.

"Charles's mother, Derek's wife, killed herself with an overdose of sleeping pills."

Olney said, "Look, Rhonda. I can't help you with this. I'm not going to tell DeeDee who she should marry and who she shouldn't. It's no business of mine who she marries."

He said, "You tell her these things yourself. You're her mother."

Millie and Melissa were back with some change for Olney. He told them they could keep it, if that was all right with their mother.

Rhonda said it was all right with her, if they would please just take it and go outside and not come back until their grandfather got home.

Another sip of his beer, then Olney said he had to go. "A couple kids are waiting for me to take them out on the lake."

She was looking down at her glass and at her fingers clasped around it. Looking like any other concerned mother who feels her daughter is about to marry someone she shouldn't.

Olney knew how she must feel. All good mothers worry about their children.

He reached out, patted her hand, told her not to worry.

"DeeDee can take care of herself. She is strong, bright, independent, and beautiful. She knows what she's doing."

Rhonda looked as if she were about to start crying.

"I can't tell DeeDee who she should or shouldn't marry, Rhonda. But if I can help any other way, I'd like to."

He said, "Sometimes if you need to borrow money, or something, let me know."

He told her of having made some money and now had no one to spend it on.

"Maybe I could buy all the kids bicycles for Christmas. Something like that."

She wasn't even listening. That was not the kind of help she wanted.

"Get DeeDee to understand that she mustn't marry Charles. That he's not good for her."

Olney said, "She will be all right, Ronda. She can handle it. Trust me."

Then he stood up. "And now I've got to go and take a couple kids fishing."

She started crying softly.

He covered her hand with his, again, for a long moment. Gave her an encouraging pat on the shoulder, and left.

It isn't easy to leave a woman when she's crying. But there wasn't anything more he could do, and he knew it.

Later there came a time when there was something he could do, and he did that. He would have felt bad if he hadn't.

Olney got back to find Cheryl and Heather there in the sunshine, with notes saying it was all right if they went fishing in the boat with Olney.

Good.

They went talking and laughing to the far end of the garden to dig worms. Olney did the digging. The girls pulled the worms out of the ground and put them into an empty can. Solomon watched. The scene could well have been a Norman Rockwell painting except that in a Rockwell painting some of the worms would have been hanging down over the edge of the can, a few of them escaping, even, and Solomon, standing there watching, would have had a bandage on one paw.

Twenty minutes later, Olney got everyone into the rowboat without anyone falling into the water. Saw that both kids had fishing poles and a supply of worms, rowed them across the lake to the west side, where the big ones were. He got himself set in the middle of the boat, a can of beer and a cigar, waiting for them to start pulling in fish for him to take off the hook.

He said, "Try to catch a lot of fish today, kids."

He said, "I want to keep busy so I can keep my mind off things I don't want to think about."

Like Rhonda crying. But he didn't say that.

"Oh, Olney."

No one said anything more for a minute or so. Then Heather said, "I think I got a bite."

And everyone watched as the bobber began to move.

Five

Dr. Whorter pointed out that the number of people growing old alone has been increasing steadily in recent years and shows no sign of leveling off any time soon. Which isn't necessarily bad, of course. Many people are quite happy to be growing old alone, that being the way they prefer to live. And, as everyone knows, people should live the way they prefer to live. When possible, anyway.

He said that his book was intended primarily for those people who are growing old alone but wish they weren't. Nice people, all of them. The kind you smile at in the line at the supermarket checkout counter, or nod to at the post office, wave to on the golf course. They glance your way across the room at the state employment office or the stockholders' meeting or the neighborhood gathering of citizens praising or protesting something or other. Maybe in the library. Wondering if you possibly are single, what you are like, wishing there were some way they could find out. You pass on the street and exchange smiles. Maybe sit across the aisle on the bus or subway, but get off at different stops or stations.

After a while it gets easier to recognize them. And, of course, if you are living alone and wish you weren't, they will recognize you, too.

These are the people who are widowed or divorced, or were never married but still hope someday to mesh their lives with someone else's under the same roof, who want to happily experience or re-experience that good feeling of waking up in the morning next to someone they are glad is there. His book is for them plus those who maybe are not living alone at the present time but have reasons to believe that they might find themselves alone in the not too distant future.

Dr. Whorter said he didn't like to think of his book as a self-help book, but he had to call it that because publishers insist that a book fall into one or another of the established categories. Otherwise, they would not know which shelf to put it on.

He said he thought of his book simply as an entertaining, thoughtful, useful collection of small psychological and philosophical insights and observations accumulated over many years, items which he had found helpful in his own efforts to understand himself as well as others. It is a very complex world we live in and we need to know all we can about what we do and why we do it.

Dr. Whorter said he was well aware of the danger in writing a self-help book. It can easily prove embarrassing.

All of us know of psychiatrists who wrote books on how to raise children properly, only to have their kids end up on drugs or in jail. Of psychologists who wrote books of advice on how to keep your marriage happy and strong, only to have their wife or husband leave them two weeks before the book came out. There are writers of health books who die young, writers of books on how to achieve financial security who go bankrupt, and salesmen of hair tonics guaranteed to provide forever a full head of healthy hair who go bald.

He said it was a risk that all writers of self-help books have to take.

It might even be, he admitted, that he would end up growing old alone himself.

Dr. Whorter's book was aimed primarily at people between the ages of forty-five and sixty-five. He wrote of the problems older people have in trying to meet eligible men or women. He gave special attention to certain aspects of the courtship period that should be kept in mind, suggested ways to adjust to people whose lifestyles were different from your own, how to reconcile differences of opinion, and how to resume a sex life after a period of abstinence.

Dr. Whorter used a lot of humor in his writing. And he openly admitted that he made up his own statistics. That, he knew, would bother a lot of people. His critics would argue that humor had no place in a serious book, and that making up your own statistics was probably illegal.

This is what Dr. Whorter had to say about that:

Which do you prefer? Do you wish to enjoy a book and at the same time be helped by it? Or is it necessary that you hang on to your stereotyped notion of what a self-help book should be like?

Do you think that everything expressed with humor is frivolous? That everything humorless is profound?

Also, he said that if anything he did helped free people from their subservience to statistics, they should be grateful.

He defended the encouragement and development of humor as an important goal for anyone seeking help from a self-help book. He warned, however, that those readers who could not tolerate humor, who get defensive when writers take a light approach to solving heavy problems, would neither enjoy nor benefit from his book.

Everyone else, he thought, would.

He said his research showed that people with a sense of humor are 78.3% less likely to end up living alone than those without a sense of humor.

He suggested that first the reader simply relax. Laugh a bit about things. Then get seriously to work on the goal they hoped to achieve: Someone to share their life with. A live-in companion.

(Although his book seemed oriented toward heterosexual relationships, he was obviously aware that many people were interested in a permanent live-in relationship with one of their own sex. His advice applied equally well to such people as to those preferring a person of the opposite sex. Either you can relate well and comfortably with someone or you can't. The problems and solutions are pretty much the same.)

He said that regardless of what other people might think, it is perfectly all right for a person of any age to actively and quite openly seek out the man or woman they feel they need and want. And don't delay. The older you get the more difficult the problem becomes.

(For some reason, Dr. Whorter tended to direct his advice toward women. He probably assumed that women would be more able to deal intelligently with the situation than men would.)

One major problem, in his opinion, was that the average unmarried middle-aged woman is still looking for that ideal man. Someone goodlooking, wealthy, in great physical condition, sexually attractive, hair graying a bit at the temples. Tall, slender, a retired professor or composer or maybe a writer. A movie star or successful industrialist with a lot of money might be acceptable, of course. Someone lonely, loving, hoping to marry again. A truly desirable man looking for a truly desirable woman.

One would guess that probably there are millions of them out there. Handsome, wealthy, truly desirable in every way. All of them searching almost desperately for that woman who is just right for them.

That, according to Dr. Whorter, simply is not true.

According to his statistics there are only eight thousand, four hundred and forty-six truly desirable unmarried men over fifty-five in the entire United States. And more than eighteen thousand truly desirable older women looking for them. In addition, according to the best data available, there are approximately fifty-six thousand and seven to eight hundred truly desirable young women also looking for them.

Dr. Whorter used a lot of clever line drawings in his book. One was a drawing of a number of older men being pursued by a large number of younger women. And behind them, quite a long way behind them, a big crowd of older women in lagging pursuit.

Dr. Whorter said that if you are a woman over fifty-five and living alone, you had better get to work. Go out on dates. Have parties. Get yourself into a busy social scene. Loosen up. Find yourself a lover. Get out and enjoy.

Most women are able to look nice and dignified at the concert or theater, he said; but the ones who end up with a man of their own are those who can look desirable and inviting across a table with candles in an intimate setting.

According to him, 98.2% of all marriage proposals between older people take place in intimate settings. Usually with wine, candles, and music. Only 1.65% over the telephone. And only 0.2% during intermission between the second and third acts at the theater, ballet, or concert. None at the opera.

Dr. Whorter had some advice on how to meet people. It is almost impossible, he said, to further an acquaintance with someone standing up. You are, for instance, quite likely to come across an eligible man or woman at the checkout counter of your local supermarket. You exchange witty remarks, smile nicely, compare opinions on the weather or the high price of food these days, recognize on each other's face the signs of loneliness and desire. But after those few amusing moments, unless one of you can somehow get the other into a sitting-down position, the two of you will walk out, get into your own cars and go your separate ways. Usually in opposite directions.

The same thing is almost certain to happen at cocktail parties, wedding receptions, or the bread and cheese table at the opening of the new art show at the local gallery.

Dr. Whorter suggested that you try something like this: "Do you mind if we sit down? I turned my ankle this morning and it is still a bit sore."

(You say, of course, that you turned your ankle while playing tennis, skiing, coming out of the bank, running the dog, jumping from the boat onto the bank, or hurrying to the store to pick up a copy of the *Wall Street Journal* before they were all sold out.)

Once you have them sitting down, Whorter suggested, get them talking about themselves. Men, especially, like to do that. If, for instance, you meet a man at the big American Legion Fourth of July party and think you might like to get to know him better, ask him what he did during the war. If he says that he was in France (or Germany, Italy, Burma, or Biloxi, Mississippi), suggest he sit down and tell you about it.

Should you meet him in the line of people signing up to collect unemployment insurance checks and he mentions that he is a musician (or architect, sculptor, writer, choreographer), comment on how difficult it must be these days for people in his line of work to make a living. And did he have time to talk about it over coffee at that little corner café.

Dr. Whorter suggested that when you meet a man for the first time, act as if you assume he is trying to pick you up. And let him get the opinion that maybe you are trying to pick him up. If he is not trying to pick you up, that will become clear enough sooner or later. And if you don't want to be picked up, not by him anyway, you can let him know that when the time comes.

First get him to show interest in you. You can later decide if you are interested in him.

Another bit of advice he offered was that a widowed or divorced woman should never hesitate to say that she had loved her late or former husband. If, of course, she really had. If the man is jealous, she might wish to make note of that. Jealousy of past relationships can be fatal to second marriages.

On the other hand, if he tells you that he loved his wife, you have learned something important. A man who once loved one woman can love again.

But be cautious, Dr. Whorter advised, of the older man who has never loved a woman. It might be that he never will. Is not able to.

Some of the things Dr. Whorter recommended would no doubt seem a bit extreme to most people.

He said that older people have the same right as younger people to do what makes them happy. Which included having sex. And for older people there are fewer worries about sex than there are for younger people. A woman past childbearing age doesn't have to worry about getting pregnant. And if she meets a man who hasn't been in bed with a woman for a while, there is less chance that she will catch anything she would need to talk to her doctor about.

So it basically comes down to a simple decision of whether two older people feel like spending the night together just for the plain enjoyment of it.

The point Dr. Whorter made was that you can have a relationship with a man without feeling that you are committing yourself to a lifetime contract. However, he recommended that you don't have an affair with someone you don't like or respect. That would cause you to lower your opinion of yourself. But don't just sit around waiting for someone to come along whom you absolutely adore. The man you are certain is absolutely and exactly the only right person in the whole world for you. If you do, Dr. Whorter cautioned, you probably will be a long time alone. If you postpone resuming your life of sex and enjoyment until that day when you finally meet that special man whom you know for sure you will love forever, you might as well get rid of your queen-size bed and buy a single.

(It would be easy to understand why some people might feel Dr. Whorter was simply trying to extend the sexual revolution to cover senior citizens. Maybe he visualized older men getting out there and persuading those middle-aged flower children to dig out that old sleeping bag and come along with them to that big demonstration in St. Petersburg, Florida, to protest cuts in Medicare, to demand higher social security benefits, and to walk along the beach in the moonlight. Lots of Bing Crosby records, music from the big band era, and maybe even a personal appearance by Perry Como.)

One complicating factor is that older people tend to be rather set in their ways. Everyone knows that. It is not likely, Dr. Whorter pointed out, that you will find another person your own age who has the same opinion on all matters as you have. But if you maintain the relationship for a while, differences will not only be modified and reconciled, but will come to be of much lesser importance than they first appeared to be.

During the getting-acquainted period, don't worry about differences of opinion on art, music, literature, favorite movie stars, or TV personalities. Young people, he pointed out, do not always agree on all such things, but that does not lead them to ask for separate rooms for the weekend at their favorite motel or beachside resort.

Everyone knows a person can learn a lot about another person simply by observing what they do and listening to what they say. Dr. Whorter said he agreed with that.

However, it is easy to be misled during the courtship period. What you have to do is keep in mind at all times that this is the courtship period and make allowances for that.

If you are getting along in years, and have been looking for a man for a while, you may be a bit impatient to get the knot tied and move in together. At the same time you are wondering if he is going to be as nice to you after you say yes as he was while you were still saying maybe.

So never let yourself forget that he is courting you. He is trying to impress you. Of course he will do things like hold the door open for you. He'd be stupid if he didn't. But what you must remember to do, should you happen to like the kind of men who hold doors open for other people, is to notice whether or not he holds the door open for people he doesn't know.

If you have grandchildren, of course he will be nice to them. He will buy them ice cream cones, take them to the circus, laugh at their jokes. That kind of thing.

You won't learn much from that. He is courting you, remember.

If it is important to you that the man you settle down with likes children, take care to notice how he treats kids other than your grandchildren. Other people's kids, or even kids of a different color or nationality. Kids in some other neighborhood or even some other part of the world.

Either he likes kids or he doesn't. That was Dr. Whorter's opinion.

Should the two of you decide to spend a week in the Bahamas to see if you are compatible and maybe also get a little sun and swimming, note whether or not he is critical and abusive. He won't be abusive to you, of course. But if he is abusive to the hotel staff, the chances are that he will end up being abusive to you once you have married and settled down on Long Island.

Dr. Whorter had some statistics relating to this kind of behavior. He said that 92.0% of the men who were abusive to hotel chefs and waitresses were later abusive to their wives and criticized their cooking.

Should you, of course, have let him know you prefer men who don't hold doors open for other people, who don't like children, and who are generally abusive and sarcastic, the same theory still applies. He is courting you, remember. Keep an eye on him. He might hold a door open for someone when he thinks you are not looking, or leave a large tip for the waitress after you've left the table, or, behind your back, try to sneak a dollar to some unhappy little kid who doesn't have money for ice cream.

Whether or not reading Dr. Whorter's book had anything to do with it, Mary would never know. But she did finally get back into the social scene. And had fun doing it.

She was lucky enough to find just the kind of man she had been looking for.

Six

Olney had finished his coffee, had lit a cigar, and was enjoying the sight of eight or ten sparrows scrambling after the doughnut fragments he had put out for them on the railing of the deck. Word had spread rapidly through the bird neighborhood that most mornings about this time some broad, dark-haired, balding man threw out some perfectly good doughnut crumbs for anyone who wanted them.

DeeDee came down with her second cup of coffee. She said, "Hi!" and settled into one of the chairs.

Olney could guess that she had something on her mind and wasn't surprised that she started right in on it.

"Mother called to say how much she enjoyed having lunch with you yesterday."

"Good. I enjoyed it too."

"She thinks you're very nice."

"I think she's nice, too. And I liked the kids."

"She talked about Charles and me, didn't she?"

"Of course."

He interrupted long enough to say that he had some doughnuts upstairs if she'd like some.

She said, "No, thanks." And went back to the subject of his lunch with her mother.

"What did she say about Charles and me?"

"She said that you are too good for Charles and that he won't treat you right and that the families of the landed gentry will look down on you because their ancestors came over on the Mayflower and yours had to walk."

Then he quickly said he was only making a joke.

"Cheryl tells me I've got to start being funnier, so now I find myself making bad jokes."

He said, "Anyway, the only feeling I got was that she is concerned about you, as any good mother should be, and wants to see you marry someone will will make you happy. That's all."

"What did you say?"

"I didn't say very much. I don't feel it is any of my business who you marry."

He re-lit his cigar. "I do remember saying that I thought you were an intelligent, attractive, and independent young woman and would be quite able to handle the situation."

She finished her coffee. Lit a cigarette.

"I'm not sure I can."

Olney watched the small birds fluttering their wings and making short hops up and down.

"And Mother is absolutely no help. She isn't even willing to talk about it. She either gets angry or insulting or starts crying."

Some unconscious reflex caused him to scratch the back of his hand and notice that it was already after nine o'clock. The girls would be coming up the driveway any moment.

"Charles tried to talk to her about it. She won't talk to him, either."

Olney nodded to show that he had heard what she said.

"Charles says he thinks it has to do with guilt feeling about my being born out of wedlock. He said she's passing on to me guilt feelings she has about herself."

Olney nodded again, took a long admiring look at the green hills and the blue sky behind them.

"That's something his father said. His father's a psychi-atrist."

All right.

"According to his father, women who have children out of wedlock feel guilty about it. They feel that society looks down on them. That's why my mother thinks Stockbridge society is going to look down on me."

Olney had never taken seriously anything psychiatrists had said about anything, but he saw no reason to bring that into the conversation. All this was strictly none of his business.

"It happened when Mother was in New York trying to become a model." She crushed out her cigarette.

"She was eighteen. Alone in New York. Struggling. Then in the spring she met a man, a student, a senior at Columbia University. From somewhere in California. Tall and blond and good looking. And they fell in love."

Olney nodded, smiled understandingly.

"He left for home when school ended, promised to write, but didn't. And two weeks after he had gone, she found that she was pregnant."

She sat there, in her tennis shoes, white shorts, T-shirt, strawberry blond hair in a ponytail, with a small frown on her face that made her look older than her eighteen years.

Nineteen, maybe.

She said, "I don't see anything about that that would make me feel ashamed of anything."

Norman Rockwell could have made use of the expres-sion on her face at that particular moment. Maybe for a picture of a beautiful young woman standing beside her automobile that is locked with the keys inside. Annoyed and frustrated. A dumb thing to do, locking yourself out of your car. But it could have happened to anyone. Noth-ing to be ashamed about.

Olney said, "I don't either. It could have happened to anyone."

"So what do you think?"

He said, "You mean about you and Charles getting married?"

"Yes."

What he thought was what he had already said. That he felt it was really none of his business.

"I don't feel it's right for me to offer any advice one way or the other."

But one thing did sort of interest him. So he asked her.

"What does Charles's father think about it? What's his opinion?"

"He thinks Charles should marry someone his own age. That I'm too young for him."

She added, "I don't agree."

Solomon moved about a bit, got to his feet, started wagging his tail. A good sign.

A moment later Olney heard the sound of a basketball being bounced up the driveway.

Before the girls got to the top of the driveway, Olney had time to repeat something he had said earlier.

"As I told your mother, DeeDee, you are an intelligent, attractive, and independent young woman and quite able to handle whatever comes along. So everything will turn out all right. Trust me."

Cheryl said, "Hi!"

Heather said, "Hi, Olney."

Olney said, "Hi, kids."

A few minutes later things were back to normal. Dee-Dee and Heather were on the court practicing layups and jump shots, Solomon had gone over to watch. Cheryl was kneeling in position at the table and asking Olney not to move so much.

The typical start of another day in the backyard of the big yellow house with blue shutters at 224 Clark Street, Stockbridge.

It was Brenda Sohmner who had written the article in the *Atlantic Monthly* many years ago about Norman Rockwell and Stockbridge. The one with the line: Stockbridge is nothing but one big Norman Rockwell fan club.

That had been eighteen or nineteen years ago. Brenda had stayed interested and involved with Stockbridge ever since. She maintained that she knew the town better than anyone else, probably.

Maybe she was right. Who knows?

She had a friend named Harry Brunnell, whom she brought to the house occasionally. Harry was in his late forties, short, a bit overweight and bald except for a fringe of short brown hair. Always a big smile, friendly greeting, and a new joke. Signs of a good salesman. He entertained the girls with sleight-of-hand tricks, like pulling a quarter out of Heather's ear and giving it to her. Or putting a coin under Cheryl's sketch pad and then making it disappear, only to show up later in her pocket.

Sometimes, when he looked tired, a suggestion of melancholy showed through. But it never lasted long.

On his second visit to the deck, late one afternoon on a hot day in July, Harry brought a contribution. A large blue insulated ice chest. Harry said it would save Olney the trouble of going in and out of his apartment all the time to get beer or Cokes. All you have to do simply fill the cooler with ice and soft drinks and cans of beer and there you are.

Olney and Harry went inside and got ice cubes and things for the cooler. Harry said he thought Olney had a good life going here and he envied him. Olney said thanks and asked Harry how business was. Harry said it was good. He was sales manager for a company that manufactured air conditioners, humidifiers, things like that. And because this was an especially hot summer, business was good.

He said he had given Brenda a window-size air conditioner for her apartment and offered to give Olney one if
he wanted it. Olney said he didn't, really, but thanks for
the generous offer.

Olney got to like Harry. Toward the end of the summer
there came the opportunity for him to do something nice
for Harry. And he did it. Of course. You always do
something nice for someone when you have the chance.

Like everyone else, Harry had a story. And Brenda, as
Olney knew she would, told it to him.

She said Harry had been born and raised in a small
town just south of Dayton, Ohio. He had been a salesman
all his life. Had never wanted to do anything else. His
father had been a salesman with a territory covering Ohio,
Indiana, and Illinois.

It was while he had a job selling audio-visual equipment to public schools in Indiana that he met and married
a young elementary-school teacher in Stephenville, a
small town east of Terre Haute. Started a family. Gradually moved on to better jobs. Made good money, worked
hard, travelled a lot. And whenever he moved on to a
bigger job in a bigger city, his family moved with him.
His wife wasn't happy about moving so often, but she did
it.

"They were living in Indianapolis," Brenda said.
"Harry was working for a big company and making good
money but on the road most of the time. Then one day his
eleven-year-old son was riding his bicycle and got hit by a
car and killed."

She said Harry was away at the time. Columbus, Ohio.
Or somewhere. It took his wife twenty-four hours to locate
him.

"That was more than she could handle. She wanted
nothing more to do with big cities. She said she was taking
their two girls and going back home to Stephenville,
where she belonged."

He did too, of course. They bought a house in Stephenville, got the girls into school, picked up the pieces of their lives. And he went back on the road again. Then one day the big opportunity of his life came along and he grabbed it.

It was a job with a brand new automotive-parts company as regional sales manager for all of New York State and Pennsylvania. He had to hire salesmen, assign territories, set up offices. It was hard work and a lot of responsibility, but he was on his way to being a rich man. Security, college money for the kids, the chance to give his wife all the luxuries of life that they had dreamed about but never had.

"He was in Philadelphia," Brenda said, "when he got word that the company had folded. He never got either the salary the company owed him or the expense money he had coming. He went home broke and depressed and tired."

And not prepared for what he found. Which was that his wife was doing rather well without him. She was back with her old classmates of high school days, had taken a small job, and was going to parties with an old friend whom she used to go out with during high school. He owned the local pharmacy. His wife had died a year or two ago.

"The girls had made friends, liked their school, refused to even consider moving anywhere else."

She said, "Harry had no idea where to look for a job or even how to try to fit into the town."

She said, "After a day or two at home he asked his wife if maybe she had actually been getting along better without him, and she admitted she sort of thought so. He asked if she was in love with her pharmacist friend, and she said she was beginning to think so."

So apparently Harry had done what seemed to him to be the honorable thing to do. He had packed his bags again and come east, ending up after a while in Pittsfield, where Brenda had met him one afternoon when he was selling an air conditioning unit in a store where she was shopping.

So it is. Everyone has a story.

Olney and Cheryl had finished working on their cartoons and now were working on a can of beer and a Coke. The afternoon was even hotter than usual but the shade had now reached nearly half way across the deck. They had earlier considered moving their chairs over into the shady part, but had decided not to. It was too hot to move. Better just to sit where they were and wait for the shade to come to them.

On the basketball court Heather and DeeDee were playing against Otis. It seemed to be about an even match.

Otis called over to ask Olney if he wanted to join them, but he had sense enough not to.

He said, "We old beer drinkers could never learn to keep our elbow in."

That wasn't bad.

"You're getting funnier, Olney."

"Thanks."

He said, "You're getting better with your drawing, too."

"Thanks."

He watched the young people playing basketball. They were all good. Even Heather. DeeDee fed her a pass under Otis's outstretched arm and she made a nice layup for a score.

After a while they left the court and came over to sit down, mop away the perspiration, and help themselves to something from the ice chest.

DeeDee said, "That's the most exercise I've had for a long time."

Otis said, "You're pretty good."

"Thanks." Then DeeDee said, "So's Heather. We make a good team."

That pleased Heather. You could tell.

Olney said he was sorry he didn't have a swimming pool so they could all get in and cool off.

Otis said he was sorry, too.

"What you might do," Olney said, "is go over to the lake and take the rowboat out and find a cool spot for a swim."

Otis looked at DeeDee. "Would you like to do that? Or are you going out?"

She said she wasn't going out. And she'd like to go.

They invited Heather, but she said she couldn't go.

"Bill's Bait Shop," Olney said. And got out his keys. "Say hello to Bill or Janet for me. Both nice people. Ask either of them to show you which boat is mine."

They went inside and got into their swimming suits and got some towels, and Olney gave then some cans of beer from the cooler to take with them.

Everyone said, "Have a good time."

Olney was watching the Red Sox lose to Detroit that night when they got back. Otis dropped off the key. He said they were late because they had stopped for dinner on the way home.

"Have a good time?"

"Yes."

"DeeDee enjoy herself?"

"She said she did."

Seven

Regardless how old a mother becomes, her feelings about her children remain the same.

If you were truly concerned about then when they were six or ten years old. you will be truly concerned about them when they are sixteen or twenty. If you went to hear your son sing in the fourth grade spring song fest because you knew it would please him to see you there, you will go some time to hear him and his group play at one of the local night clubs.

Same thing.

Mary didn't like the kind of music Gregory and his friends played or the kind of places they played in. The noise and heavy smoke were bearable only because she knew she wouldn't have to stay long.

When she did go, which was not very often, he always saved her a seat at the table where he and the others sat during the break so he could introduce them to her. She always told them they sounded great. Once, one of them, the one who played that awful instrument that they use instead of a piano, asked if there was anything she'd like to hear.

She said, "How about something by Berlioz?"

Which got a laugh. And which also established something in her favor.

In much the same spirit, she had gone with her daughter a time or two to listen to a speaker who her daughter said was especially worth hearing. Or to a panel discussion on some aspect of the New Woman and her role in the changing world.

Pauline had herself once given a talk on sexual harassment in the workplace, and had managed to work in a few kind words about her mother for supporting her in her efforts to find independence.

All right.

She couldn't remember anything she had done or said that deserved any special praise, but if it pleased her daughter she was glad she had done or said it.

And although she didn't like the idea of going all the way down to Stockbridge for lunch, Mary went to the Red Lion Inn every once in a while so Rosemary could introduce her to the other waitresses she worked with. All nice friendly young people.

Either you like your kids or you don't. Dr. Whorter would have agreed with that.

Because Mary's copy of Dr. Whorter's book had no dust jacket, there was no way of knowing what he looked like or how old he was. No other previous publications were listed, so she assumed that this was his only book.

Whether young or old, he obviously felt kindly toward older people. He advised that no one get into a panic just because he or she has reached sixty. Things don't get worse. Maybe better, even. Although you are not as involved in as many things as you once were, your total amount of intensity remains the same as before. He said you could quote him on that. He said you could refer to it as Whorter's Law.

Whorter's Law is this:

The importance and intensity attached to any one thing or experience increases in direct proportion to the decreasing number of things or experiences available.

When in the cold of late winter the wood pile dwindles and the pieces of kindling get fewer and fewer, the more valuable each log or stick of kindling becomes.

For an older person on a small, fixed income, finding an item on sale that you were going to have to buy anyway gives you that same kind of excited happy feeling that you got back when you were young and had more money and got a really good buy on a great used car.

The less often you get invited to a really good party, the more excited you are about being invited to a really good party when one comes along.

Finally remembering where you left your reading glasses is a happy feeling that bears comparison to that time when you had almost given up hope of finding that brand new golf ball when you suddenly spotted it in the thick grass of the rough to the right of the fairway on the fourth hole of some golf course somewhere. Or like the time you wanted to take your date to a movie but didn't have any money, then found a ten dollar bill in an old sport jacket you hadn't worn for a while.

That kind of thing.

He said it was not a perfect law. Few laws are.

About 24%, according to his research.

Sometimes when Mary's neighbor, Florence, came over to sit in the yard, Mary read some things from Dr. Whorter's book that she thought Florence might be interested in. Although Florence had shown no interest at all in ever again acquiring a male live-in companion, Mary suspected that Florence would not turn down the opportunity for one should it come along. And probably, though she wouldn't admit it, would love to see it happen.

So from time to time she offered Dr. Whorter's opinions on things a woman should keep in mind should she actually be looking for a man, and how to recognize the right one should she meet him.

Different kinds of women are looking for different kinds of men. The kind of woman who is hoping someday to meet a professional football player or boxing promoter or race track owner is different from the kind of woman who hopes someday to find a romantic poet or forest ranger or Salvation Army captain.

Dr. Whorter suggested that no woman over fifty years old try to kid herself into thinking that she can change her personality in order to conform to some man's preference. Should you happen to be sort of shy and chance to meet a nice man who definitely prefers women who are aggressive and outgoing, his advice was that you accept the fact that you are shy and look around a little harder for a man who sort of likes shy women. Otherwise, you might have to go through the rest of your life trying to pretend to be something you are not. And if you tend to be a bit too rigid and uncompromising, don't despair. There are men that way, too. And they are looking for someone like themselves. Rigid and uncompromising.

Don't try to make big personality changes. Just look harder.

No one is perfect. But you don't have to be perfect to be loved. Everyone is different in one way or another. Perfectionist, cautious, conformist, thrifty, judgmental, strict, and so forth. Or maybe carefree, spendthrift, reckless, rebellious, accepting, forgiving, and so forth. Just be careful not to match yourself with someone too different from yourself. Nor, in some cases, someone too similar.

Two thrifty and conservative people might live together quite comfortably. Two demanding and judgmental people might not.

Two loving people could. Two domineering people couldn't.

If you meet a man who tells you he loves you just the way you are, you might wish to give that some careful thought. Make sure you know what he means. It may be he is making unfair demands. If, for instance, he means that he likes your slender figure and long black hair, that could be a problem should you put on weight or your black hair get gray lines through it. Of, if he wants you to stay always the aggressive and successful businesswoman you now are, that would mean trouble should you decide next year to quit the business world to write children's stories or become a social worker.

If, however, should that person mean he likes you just the way you are, which is kind, loving, understanding, charitable, witty, intelligent, and so forth, and those are characteristics you hadn't planned to change anyway, then having someone love you just the way you are is not risky at all.

Florence didn't seem to be especially interested in any of Dr. Whorter's ideas. She was a bit too conventional in her thinking to accept easily Dr. Whorter's rather radical approach to the fact of getting old.

She went Sunday mornings to some medical center up in Pittsfield to hear some specialist discuss some particular health problem common to older people. And that afternoon came over to Mary's yard to talk about it.

"Arthritis: What It Is and How to Live with It."

Mary said, "But you don't have arthritis.'

That, as Florence pointed out, was beside the point. Maybe the subject was "Living with Diabetes."

Florence didn't have diabetes, either.

Afterwards, all those who had attended the lecture went to the hospital cafeteria for lunch and all senior citizens got a 35% discount on their meal and a small stack of brochures from nursing homes and private medical plans.

Florence said, "At least it's a good way to meet people."

"It may be a good place to meet people," Mary said. "But probably a poor place to go looking for a tennis partner."

Florence's answer to that was that the tennis champion of Elwood, South Carolina, was sixty-two years old.

"But you don't play tennis."

That, too, was beside the point.

Mary had some statistics from Dr. Whorter she thought Florence might be interested in.

Of those women over fifty-five, living alone and looking for a good man, more than 80% meet between three and four good eligible men every year but do not recognize them. Moreover, more than 69% would not know a good man if they saw one. (For men, the figure is much worse. Dr. Whorter said that 84% of those men who say they are looking for a good woman wouldn't recognize a good woman even if she came up and held the door open for him and offered to buy him a drink and dinner, do his income tax for him, and help him pick out some better looking clothes.)

Mary asked Florence if she were interested in hearing Dr. Whorter's thoughts on the difference between accepting a person's faults and overlooking them.

Florence said she wasn't.

One afternoon when Florence was over visiting, her daughter, Meg, stopped by. Meg, who looked a lot like her mother, was tall and slender, wore blue jeans and work boots. She and a partner had a small landscaping business. A strong and independent young woman who reminded Mary of her daughter, Rosemary. She was on her way somewhere, but had time to stay for a glass of wine and to say some unsettling things.

Mary happened to be reading Dr. Whorter's book at the time and asked Meg if she had read it.

She hadn't, but quickly glanced through it, read a bit of it, said she didn't like it.

She said it was out of date.

"Women, even older women, don't chase men anymore. Men would like to believe they do, but they don't."

"He doesn't suggest chasing them," Mary said. "He was simply suggesting ways to find one, should you want one. And how to recognize a good one from a bad one."

Mary said, "He thinks it's perfectly all right for a woman to grow old alone if she wants to. He even talks about the many advantages of living alone."

Meg pointed out that just because a woman doesn't want to be married doesn't mean that she plans to live alone for the rest of her life.

"It is not a matter of either living with a man or living alone."

All right. Mary understood.

Meg laughed at the part where Dr. Whorter said that one of the nice things about life is to wake up in the morning next to someone you're glad is there.

"Most married women wake up in the morning wishing they were alone. Or with someone else."

She had been married once and knew what she was talking about.

"Having a man is all right," she said. "If you want one. Be in love, even, if you wish. But you don't have to commit yourself to one person for the rest of your life."

Mary said, "Of course not. I suppose. Unless you want to."

It seemed hardly important enough to even bother to disagree, but Mary did point out that many creatures mated for life. And she mentioned wolves as one example, recalling an article she had read on that subject only two days ago.

"Wolves don't get married," Meg said. "They may decide to take one mate for life, but that is it. They don't have a ceremony. She doesn't give up her own name and take his. And if later she decides to go her own way, she doesn't have to hire a wolf lawyer to ask some wolf judge if it is all right to do so."

According to the article Mary had read, wolves do have a wedding ceremony. Something about them going around a certain area marking the edge of their territory. Pausing a moment here and a moment there. Passing along the information that they were now doing things together.

Mary couldn't think of a way to say that without sounding crude.

"I think they have their own kind of ceremony," Mary said.

Then she asked Meg to tell her more about her landscaping business.

Meg preferred to say some more things about marriage.

"It's an old-fashioned idea that all women want to get married and have children. Some do and some don't."

She said, "Society won't let a woman have babies and a career at the same time. And more and more women are choosing just the career."

Florence took the opportunity to get in a jab of her own.

"A lot of young men aren't getting married either."

She said, "You told me once you wondered if your son, Gregory, would ever get married."

All right. Enough.

Mary finished the rest of her wine and gradually got the conversation onto another subject.

The idea that a woman in her thirties might not want someday to get married and have children was unsettling. Mary hoped that Pauline didn't feel that way. She wasn't yet ready to settle for having only one grandchild.

To put her mind at ease, she found an excuse to call Pauline that evening and ask how things were going.

"Your Aunt Sylvia called yesterday," Mary said. "She asked about you."

Which happened to be true.

Pauline asked about Aunt Sylvia and was told that she was fine.

The next part wasn't really true.

"She asked if you planned on getting married again and having children. I told her I didn't know, of course. That being your business, not mine. I said that I assumed you still planned to have a family, but that we had never discussed the matter."

And she waited.

Pauline said, "Who knows?"

Then she said she was glad Mary had called because she wanted to tell her that her softball team was playing tomorrow evening, and would Mary like to come out to watch.

All right.

Mary said she'd be there. Of course.

If you care enough to go to their first piano recital in the third grade, you care enough to go watch them play third base when they are thirty-six.

Mary Ostrowski every once in a while lost a pupil, gained a pupil, gave one away.

She had been giving lessons to the seven-year-old daughter of a black couple she knew slightly who lived not far from her, a talented child who after only nine months had gone through the music books that would have taken the average child three years.

She told the mother that.

"She needs the best teacher you can find. And you can find teachers better than me."

The child's mother was not prepared for this. She had arranged for piano lessons for her daughter for the same reasons other parents did. All her neighbors did it. It's the thing to do. When the kids are old enough to sit up straight at the piano, you give them lessons.

"I will work with her for the rest of the summer," Mary said, "but in September she must start at the School of Music and take lessons from a really good teacher."

The woman said she thought Mary was a good teacher. Her husband thought so, too. And her daughter liked her.

"That's nice. But we are not dealing with something so simple as whether or not the pupil likes her teacher."

She said, "There are some things in life that are much too important to be dealt with lightly. And this is one of them."

She gave the mother a hard and almost unfriendly look.

"Your daughter has the potential in music that is so great that if you do not provide her with the means to develop it to her maximum ability, I will never forgive you nor let you forgive yourself."

All right, all right. For God's sake!

"I have friends at the school. I'll talk to them, and I'll tell you next week when she is to start."

"Thank you."

Mary looked around. What she saw indicated that these were people of good taste and above-average income.

"If you feel that she needs a scholarship, I'll see that she gets one."

The woman didn't say anything. You could tell by the look on her face that all she wanted at this time was for her husband to get home so she could talk to him about how their music teacher had suddenly gone wild.

Mary started for the door. Then turned around.

"And you must get the piano tuned."

The woman said she'd do that.

"I'll see you next week."

Instead of going straight home, she drove down to Lenox and stopped in at the bookstore to tell the nice woman behind the desk that she had enjoyed the book by Dr. Whorter.

The lady remembered. "Did you ever decide whether it was humor or psychology?"

Mary said she thought it was a bit of both.

She bought two books before she left. One about the changing life styles among today's youth, and the other a novel by a local author that the lady recommended.

Mary enjoyed watching the softball game. The score was close and Pauline played well. In the top of the last inning Pauline hit a double with a runner on base and the score was tied. The next batter hit a long fly ball and Pauline was able to score. The next batter hit a pop fly and the side was out, leaving Pauline's team one run ahead going into the last half of the ninth inning. If the other team didn't score, Pauline's team would win.

Mary had never paid much attention to baseball before. She hadn't realized that baseball games could actually be exciting. In a way.

Things began to get noisy. The other team got two players on base with only one out. The next batter grounded out, but moved the runners to second and third. So there were two outs and two on.

Unfortunately, the woman coming to the plate was the big outfielder, probably their best hitter. She did as expected. She hit the first pitch far out into left field and it looked as if the game was lost. But the left fielder on Pauline's team ran a long way and caught the ball over her shoulder.

Everyone went crazy. Jumping up and down and yelling. Leaping up and hitting their open palms against other players' open palms and everyone jumping on everyone else. It took a long time for things to calm down. Then the players of both teams got in line and shook hands with the players of the other team.

Pauline's teammates told Mary how much they appreciated her coming out to watch the game. They invited her to join them at a little tavern nearby for a victory beer or two, but she said maybe some other time.

After dinner in her side yard she had a glass of wine and read some of the novel she had bought. Then went inside and watched part of an old movie on TV. While she was doing that she got a call from an old friend over in Amherst asking if Mary could come for lunch tomorrow.

Sure.

The caller was a former professor Mary had studied under many years ago. She was now in her seventies and lived alone and felt forgotten and unimportant. Tonight she had gotten lonely. She needed someone to talk to about those earlier years when she was young and popular and pursued by ardent lovers.

It would not be exactly an exciting afternoon and certainly not something to look forward to, but Mary said she would do it.

"I have some lessons in the morning, but I could get there by one-thirty. If that's not too late."

That would be fine.

"But plan to stay for a while because I have a lot I want to talk to you about."

All right.

As a result of doing that nice thing, spending a boring afternoon in Amherst trying to make an old lady feel better, a nice thing happened to Mary on her way home.

The first nice thing that had happened to her for a while.

Eight

Cheryl's mother came by one morning to say hello.

Olney was out in back. He had been working in the garden for a while and was now standing by the deck, admiring it. Running his hands along the railing. Reminiscing.

The deck had an importance to Olney beyond being simply a place to sit and entertain friends. At least once a day he took time to examine it for splinters or cracks, none of which he ever found. It was a solid and beautiful construction, fifteen by twenty feet, made of pressure-treated pine with that faint greenish-copper gleam. Two by six boards a quarter inch apart. Railings four by four with two by six cap, two by four horizontals. Six by six supports into the ground. He remembered the planning of it and the building of it as if it were only yesterday.

Forty years from now this deck would still be standing and in good condition. Which was the way Olney wanted it. Some might wonder why a person Olney's age might want to build something to last forty years when he himself would likely have no more than five or ten. But he had built it to last, anyway.

Someday, someone sitting here would say that whoever had built this deck years ago had certainly done a good job.

He wouldn't want it any other way.

Cheryl's mother said, "Hi!"

So did Olney.

She was about thirty years old, a bit heavier than she should have been, had a nicely rounded friendly face with a happy expression on it, and was carrying an armful of bright colored flowers. For Olney, apparently.

"You're Olney, aren't you?"

He said he was. And she said she was Cheryl's mother and her name was Rosemary.

She had come to tell him that Cheryl and Heather wouldn't be up to see him today because she had taken them up to Pittsfield to spend the day with Cheryl's grandmother.

She was wearing blue jeans, sandals, T-shirt, and looked casual and relaxed, so Olney didn't mind that he looked a bit scruffy himself.

She said that the flowers were from her garden.

"You're always sending Cheryl home with vegetables, so I thought it was time that I brought you something."

He thanked her. Asked if she had time to sit down for a while and she said she did.

She had introduced herself as Rosemary Heddon, so he asked her if she were related to the Heddon people who made fishing lures. She said she wasn't. Not as far as she knew. Her former husband's family had had a lot of money, but they hadn't made it selling fishing lures.

"It's good of you to let Cheryl and Heather spend so much time up here." She said, "You've been a big help to them."

He said he thought it was more the other way around.

"They've been good company. I don't know what I'd have done without them."

"They are a couple of troubled kids. They really needed someone like you."

All right. But he told her he had never thought of them as troubled kids. They both seemed like mature and intelligent young people.

"Cheryl is much too serious for her age. And withdrawn. And Heather is a thirteen-year-old who should be with girls her own age, And with boys."

Olney said, "Maybe so. But they seem to be happy together, and good friends."

He asked if Cheryl got her artistic talents from her mother, and Rosemary said no. "But her teachers say she is very talented."

"I think so, too."

Rosemary said, "All she wants to do is draw. Something she learned to do for the wrong reasons."

Olney waited.

"She learned to draw back when she was going through rough times because I was going through rough times myself. It was something she taught herself to do."

She said, "Drawing was her way of escaping from the arguments going on. My husband and I fighting and yelling at one another. Drawing was her security blanket. Sometimes you could go up to her when she was drawing and call her name and she wouldn't even hear you."

"She's really good," Olney said. "She's better at drawing than I am at being funny."

"Have you ever noticed that when she's sketching, you can speak to her and she won't even hear you?"

He said he hadn't.

"Usually she just says not to move so much. Or face the other way."

Rosemary said, "She never goes anywhere without her sketch pad. Until just a few weeks ago she used to take it to bed with her."

Olney scratched a spot on the back of his hand. Then he reached into Harry's ice chest and got out a can of beer.

It was a little early for a beer, but he wanted one anyway. He offered Rosemary one, but she said it was too early.

She said, "One thing about Cheryl that worries me is that she hates school. She says she's going to drop out when she's sixteen."

"She won't," Olney said. "Trust me. I said the same thing when I was her age."

He said, "This is summer, remember. Every kid hates school during summer vacation. That's what summer vacations are for."

He took a sip of the beer.

"When I was a kid the principal kept the back door locked every nice day in spring because of me."

That got a small laugh.

Then she said, "There's something you should know about Heather."

Olney scratched the back of his hand again. And wondered if he was beginning to get more impatient in his old age than he used to be.

He said, "I don't need to know anything more about Heather than I already know."

She said, "The woman Heather lives with is not her grandmother, but her foster mother. Heather is a ward of the state. Her father's in jail and her mother's an alcoholic."

She added another fact or two.

"The foster mother is getting old and Heather won't be able to stay with her much longer. She will have to move to another home. Or be adopted."

It was probably because of getting old. Older people aren't as patient as they once were.

He stood up. He said, "I almost forgot. I wanted to give you some things from the garden. Do you want to come down and help me pick out some things for you?"

All right.

He led the way. They picked some tomatoes and beans and other things. Then Olney got a paper bag from the apartment to put them in.

He said he hoped she'd stop by any time she felt like it. She said she would.

"Cheryl and Heather will be up to see you tomorrow, I'm sure."

"Good. I'd miss them if they didn't."

He said that should she sometime pass by the house and he wasn't here, she should feel free to help herself to anything in the garden she wanted.

She said she'd do that, and thanks.

He walked with her down to the end of the driveway and they said good-bye.

On the way back up, Olney said he didn't know whether he should work in the garden some more or go fishing.

He asked Solomon's opinion.

"What do you think? Work in the garden or go fishing?"

You could easily tell what Solomon thought. Gardening bored him.

So they went fishing. Olney got a few cans of beer and a pocketful of cigars and they headed for Bill's Bait Shop.

A lot of men envy Bill Ferguson. And not just because of his good-looking blond wife, Janet.

If, at the end of a boring day's work behind a stupid desk in some dumb office you happen to be driving along Route 7 past Laurel Lake in Lee and chance to look down toward the water, you will see a dock and some boats. That's Bill's Bait Shop. Back from the water about fifty yards is a small house, red with gray trim, where Bill and Janet live. They have lived there for years. They could sell the house and lake frontage any time they wanted to and have money enough to retire to Florida and live well. But, as Bill says, what the hell they'd do in Florida, he'd never know. They'd be bored to death.

"Here at least you got the excitement of having to stay awake at night to keep people from stealing your boats."

Bill was Olney's age, give or take a year or two. He was a lean and wiry man with short gray hair, and always with a short stubble of whiskers that made it look every day as if he hadn't shaved for two or three.

Olney told Bill he needed to go out in the rowboat for a while to get away from things.

"Like who, for instance?"

Olney said, "Why don't you get Janet to watch the shop for a while and join me?"

Bill had better sense than that.

"You aren't going to catch anything out there in the hot sun this time of day."

He suggested Olney sit on the dock and they talk for a while. So they did that. Olney gave Bill one of his beers and one of the cigars.

Bill said that another reason he didn't want to go out on the lake right now was that Janet was having one of her heavy drinking days and he didn't want to leave her alone to take care of customers.

"If she has a drinking problem." Olney said, "there's no need for you to tell me about it."

"I almost fell off this dock once, laughing at her trying to catch two dozen minnows for a couple summer tourists. Trying to scoop them out of the tank and get them into a bucket of water for two wide-eyed summer types. She would chase the little things up and down the tank, yelling when she caught one."

He said, "They must'a thought she was crazy, and I'm sure it was something they talked about when they got back to the city."

And he told about the time she was in her cups and tried to count out two dozen night crawlers for a local politician and his wife. She kept losing count and throwing them all back and starting all over again.

"She's a good woman," Olney said. "We all have our little problems."

"Her old man was a real alcoholic."

All right.

"Spent all his time in bars. Couldn't hold onto a job. Brought his drunken friends home and kept everyone awake all night with their drinking and singing."

He said, "She was so embarrassed by the way the old man behaved that when she was in high school she wouldn't bring her friends to the house."

Bill took another puff on the cigar and threw the rest of it into the water.

"She said her father ruined her life. And she hates him."

After a moment, he added another thought.

"Every time something reminds her of him, she gets mad all over again and starts hitting the bottle."

Olney said he thought he'd go out on the lake for an hour or so, anyway. Just for the hell of it.

Bill got him a cold beer from the refrigerator to take with him.

"But you won't catch anything."

Which proved to be true.

When Olney got back to the dock an hour later, Bill said, "I knew you wouldn't."

Olney said, "I should have listened to you."

"You can't catch fish in the middle of the day," Bill said.

"You're right."

On the way home Olney said to Solomon, "It's not as much fun when the kids aren't along."

Olney got back to the patio to find Brenda relaxing in one of the chairs, her feet up on another. She had a gin and tonic, a cigarette, and a favor to ask.

First, she asked if he'd been fishing and he said he had.

"Catch anything?"

"You can't catch anything in the middle of a hot day in August."

She was sorry to hear that.

Then she said that Sunday was Harry's birthday and she'd like to do something nice for him.

"What I'd like to do, if you don't mind, is have some cake and coffee and ice cream here on the deck Sunday afternoon."

Olney's only objection was that that wasn't really enough for a birthday party.

He said, "How about having hot dogs and hamburgers and potato chips. Things like that."

She liked that. Harry would love it.

"You get the cake and candles and ice cream. I'll take care of everything else."

She offered to give him the money for it, but he said he wouldn't take it.

He said, "I like Harry. The least I can do is help have a good party for him."

He said, "I'm sentimental about birthday parties. I came from a big family and whenever anyone had a birthday, that was always a big occasion."

He said, "Some things in life are important and some are not. Things like birthday parties, graduation, weddings, anniversaries, thing like that are important."

He said, "Most other things aren't."

On the patio that evening, watching the sunset and having his last cigar and beer of the day, Olney thought some more about the party for Harry. It would be fun, of course, but for him some things would be missing. Such as a couple old friends. A woman partner. And a number of people he was close to and would see again from time to time. People his own age.

He remembered something a man named Tennyson had said to him once.

What Tennyson had said was that you don't make old friends after fifty. And after fifty it isn't easy to find the right woman, either. And the older you get the more difficult it becomes.

Last October, when Olney was on his way home after visiting his kids in California, his plane had been delayed in Chicago because a heavy fog had closed the airport for a while. He had sat at the bar in the cocktail lounge waiting for the weather to clear, and had got into a conversation with a man named John Tennyson. They had both been overhearing the bartender explain to a waitress the reason why a man at a nearby table had been sitting there a long time doing not much more than stare into his drink. He happened to be an artist and a rather good one. He was being evicted from the apartment he had lived in for nearly ten years because the building was being converted into a condominium. The landlord was his brother-in-law. His wife and kids had gone to stay with her mother until he found a new place to live.

Tennyson looked over at Olney.

"Everyone has a story."

Olney liked that. That was a good line. He said, "I guess you're right."

The man said, "Everyone would like to believe that they are the only one whose life would make a good novel."

They introduced themselves, shook hands. and Tennyson asked if he could buy Olney a drink.

He said, "It's my policy that if you meet a man at a bar, you buy him a drink."

That being the man's policy, Olney said he'd go along with it.

He said, "I'm sorry we didn't meet in a place where they sold automobiles."

Tennyson was short, bearded, wore dark-rimmed glasses. He asked Olney what he did for a living and

Olney said he was a retired plumber. Tennyson didn't say what he did for a living. Olney assumed he was a writer or professor.

He asked Olney where he was from and Olney said Stockbridge, Massachusetts, and Tennyson said he knew where that was. He'd been there. Before his wife died four years ago they had gone up there once or twice a year just to get away from the city. Stayed at the Red Lion Inn.

Olney was sorry to hear that Tennyson's wife had died, and told him that. He said that his own wife had died not long ago.

That sort of set the tone for the rest of the conversation. Tennyson was on his way out to Sacramento to the funeral of his younger brother. He talked about his younger brother's death and of the problems his sister-in-law was going to have.

"The only real tragedy we know, Olney, is the death of someone near and dear to us who dies ahead of their allotted time. Wife, children, siblings. A death for which neither you nor they were responsible."

He took a long thoughtful sip of his drink.

"The Greeks had it all wrong," he said. "A man kills his father and marries his mother and they call that tragedy. All he did was suffer the consequences of his own anger and foolishness."

He said, "If Oedipus had passed that crossroad half an hour earlier or later, few people today would ever have heard of him."

Olney said that even though the man did happen to pass the crossroad when he did, Olney still hadn't heard of him. He asked who Oedipus was. And signalled to the bartender for another drink apiece.

Tennyson said it was only a story. Hardly worth telling.

Olney said that when his wife had died the doctor kept saying that there hadn't been anything anyone could do.

"That," said Tennyson, "is tragedy."

Their drinks came and for a minute or two they sipped their drinks and looked out the window at the thick fog. Then they started talking and for half an hour or more covered most of the subjects that seemed important.

"Sometimes I wish my life had been different and I had gone to college and learned more about the Greeks and who Oedipus was. Things like that."

Tennyson said, "You're all right, Olney. I'm sure you were a good plumber."

"I was a real good plumber," Olney said. "But knowing the things a plumber knows isn't the same as knowing what a professor knows. Or a poet."

"And vice versa."

He took another sip of his drink and added another thought.

"If you were a good plumber, you would also have been a good poet or professor."

He spoke with all the confidence of a person who has had a few drinks.

"A bad plumber and you would have also been a bad poet or professor."

All right.

After a while the fog began to thin a bit. The low dark clouds weren't quite so low and dark. You could see almost all the way to the end of the field. They heard the sound of one engine starting up.

"You're a good man, Olney."

"Thanks."

Olney told Solomon he thought it was time to call it a night. He had to get up early to go over to Northampton and take an old friend out fishing.

"The old man used to work for me. Doesn't get around very well anymore. The least I can do is take him out fishing every once in a while."

The Red Sox weren't playing. But he watched a bit of the Yankees-Tigers game.

Taking the old friend out fishing was a nice thing to do. And because he did it, something nice happened to him in return.

Nine

Mary Ostrowski met Olney in the parking lot of the Sanderston Inn. She was on her way back to Pittsfield after spending an exhausting afternoon with her old friend and former teacher in Amherst, listening patiently to a prolonged reminiscence of years past when she was young, beautiful, talented, loved by her students and pursued by ardent lovers.

Sanderston is halfway between Amherst and Pittsfield. It is just off Route 20, the same road Olney used in returning from Northampton to Stockbridge. It is by that kind of coincidence and luck that they happened to meet.

Sanderston is a rather ordinary little village that few people know even exists. Not much there except a gas station, general store, small church and small school. Things like that. Plus one really delightful little inn with good food, congenial atmosphere, comfortable lounge, a long bar and a spacious dining room. Two large fireplaces, and three guest rooms upstairs. Most people who know of the place are willing to go a mile or two out of the way to stop in for dinner or a drink.

It was dusk, a light rain falling, and Mary forgot and left her parking lights on. She was walking from the parking lot toward the entrance when she heard a man calling.

"Hey, Lady."

She turned around.

"You left your lights on."

He was right. She saw that.

"Want me to turn them off for you?"

She would, of course.

Nice of him to do that. She waited by the door for him to get there so she could tell him so.

She said, "Thank you. That was nice of you." And held the door open for him.

He was a big man, broad, a bald spot on top of his head that she would likely not have noticed except that he brushed some hair across it as he approached. A sort of rough and weatherbeaten workingman's face, but a nice smile.

He said, "You're welcome." Then added what she assumed was to make her feel better, "I often do that myself."

They smiled once more at one another. Then he held the inner door open for her.

Simply one of those nice little things that happen all the time. Two nice people meet and at no cost or inconvenience to either, share a pleasant experience that provides a momentary warm feeling for both. Always good to be able to do something helpful for someone else. And vice versa.

Mary walked into the restaurant.

An attractive young woman with long blond hair, a pretty smile, and menus cradled in her arms had positioned herself just inside the door. She greeted them politely and asked if they had come for dinner.

Now this was a different situation.

Mary, of course, had come for dinner. But having a dinner partner more or less thrust upon her was another matter.

The young hostess waited. Smiled again, and after a moment, thinking they perhaps had not heard the question, repeated it.

"Are you having dinner?"

Mary hoped the man behind her would say no, that he was only on his way to the bar. She turned and looked at him, a bit impatiently.

He brushed some hair across his bald spot. Looked at the hostess. And after a moment, said, "Yes."

That brought a nice smile to the young woman's face. She appeared pleased that they had reached a decision. She asked them to follow her, and led them quickly toward the dining room before they changed their minds.

Mary had no choice but to follow.

The hostess led them to a table by the window, one with a view of the brook behind the inn and of the woods behind it.

"Is this all right?"

They both said it was, of course. They said it was fine. Which it was.

She gave each of them a menu and said that a waitress would be right with them.

What had only moments ago been a slight drizzle suddenly became a downpour, and a curtain of rain came between them and the view that would have been so nice to look at.

A waitress appeared and asked if they would like cocktails before dinner. Mary said she would. And ordered a martini.

Her companion, still looking uncomfortable, brushed some hair across his bald spot and ordered a bottle of beer.

Mary had been carrying a book to read while having dinner. She put it on the window ledge beside her.

They introduced themselves. He mumbled his full name and she didn't quite get it. But he said he liked to be called Olney. Which was all she needed.

She wasn't sure that he heard her last name, but no difference. Olney and Mary. They shook hands and picked up the menus, studied them in silence for a while.

She suddenly realized how tense and tired she was. The afternoon had been a strain. Listening to an old woman parade in front of herself ghosts of former friends and lovers can be wearying.

She had looked forward to a quiet and relaxing little meal, her book propped up so she could read it as she ate. She felt a surge of self-disapproval at letting herself get caught up in something she had not wanted and probably would not enjoy. She wondered if it were still possible to correct the situation some way.

She should simply have said to the hostess that they were not together.

Then in a sudden reversal, she upbraided herself for even considering the possibility of appearing rude and hurting the man's feelings.

"They gave us a nice table," she said. "Don't you love the view?"

Unfortunately, because of the rain, they could no longer see the view. But he said he liked it, too.

She could see that he felt uncomfortable, and felt bad about that.

"Having dinner with someone is always better than eating alone, don't you think?"

That got a smile, but not much else. Apparently, he wasn't very talkative.

He was casually dressed. A little too casually, actually. Worn and faded blue jeans, a checkered flannel shirt not buttoned up all the way. No tie. He must have noticed her appraisal because he buttoned the shirt up one more button. Then apologized.

"I'm not exactly dressed for dinner," he said. "I've been out fishing."

She protested, "You're dressed perfectly all right, I assure you."

"I hope I'm not embarrassing you."

"Of course not."

Then, because she had to say something, she asked. "Did you catch any fish?"

He had. You could tell by the big grin on his face.

"Some beauties!"

A beauty is a large fish, apparently.

"I was fishing with an old friend. I gave him the fish. He'll be eating well for a while."

She asked, "Where did you fish?"

"The Connecticut River."

"Northampton?"

"Yes. The Oxbow. Know where that is?"

She did. She said she had some friends on Oxbow Road.

"Have you ever visited the Audubon Sanctuary there?"

He said he hadn't.

He drank his beer with a look of real satisfaction. And she smiled. A nice working man who fished, enjoyed his beer, no doubt watched baseball games on TV at the neighborhood bar.

She sipped her martini and wondered what to say next. They would have to talk about something.

"Do you come here often?"

"Once or twice a year."

After a moment or two, she asked, "Do you mind if I ask what you do for a living?"

He said that he was a retired plumber, which was about what she would have guessed.

"That sounds like an interesting occupation, Olney. I hope you enjoyed it and made a lot of money."

He said he had. He ended up owning a plumbing-supply business. One of the biggest in Northampton, had bought the building it was in and the one next to it. Both of which had become much more valuable by the time he sold them.

"You were more than just a plumber, then. You were a businessman."

He preferred to think of himself as a plumber. A good one.

He said, "Anyone can own a plumbing-supply business. Even if he doesn't know a pipe wrench from a knee joint. But it takes a lot of time and hard work to become a good plumber."

All right.

The waitress came to see what they would like to order for dinner. Mary noticed that Olney had finished his beer and was looking at her as if he were wondering whether she would be offended or scared or something should he order another.

She said, "I don't care for another martini, but if you want another drink I'm sure there would be time before dinner comes."

He said he thought maybe he would. Now that she'd mentioned it.

After the waitress left, Mary said, "If this is not too personal a question, Olney, could I ask how old you are?"

He said he was sixty-five.

He said he had started as a plumber's helper right after graduating from Northampton High School. Then had got his old job back after getting home from the war.

She asked, of course, where he had been stationed.

He had been in the Italian campaign. U.S. Infantry. Had gone onto Anzio Beach with the first wave.

"Were you scared?"

"Very much."

"You must have been very young at the time."

"I was. But I had a brother even younger, who went into the army about the same time I did."

That got him started talking. Memories of childhood. Of a large and happy family, games and jokes and good times. Not much money, unfortunately. Of a father born on a farm, who then worked most of his life on the railroad back in the days when you didn't make much money working for the railroad.

He had married the girl he had gone with in high school. He had two children, both married and now living in California.

He said that his wife had died over a year ago. Nearly a year and a half, in fact. They had been married for forty-two years.

"I would guess that you were no doubt a faithful husband. If that is not too personal a comment."

He had been. He said, "I don't know why one man would need more than one woman. But that's only my opinion."

Did he live alone? He said he did.

"Do you go out much with women on dates? Or go to parties?"

He said he didn't know many women. And didn't like parties.

She realized that she was sitting across from a man who probably hadn't spent a night in bed with a woman for nearly a year and a half.

She looked at him and tried to picture how he would look in a suit with a shirt and tie, and decided he would look all right.

A bit uncomfortable, but all right.

He had ordered a steak. She the chef's salad. He asked if she'd like part of his steak. She said thanks, took part of what he offered, offered part of her salad in return. He said he didn't often eat salad, but he'd take some of hers because she had been kind enough to offer it.

For a while they just ate and looked out the window at the rain. The heavy rain. And suddenly she remembered something.

"Oh dear!"

"What's the matter?"

"I think I left a window open in my car."

He said, "The window on the driver's side was up. I remember checking that when I turned your lights off."

"The other side. The passenger side."

He put down his fork and said he'd go check.

"It's not necessary, Olney. A little rain won't hurt that much."

She said, "I'm sorry I mentioned it."

He got up. "If I don't check it, it will be on your mind and spoil your dinner."

She watched him leave. Saw him stop by the front door and say something to the hostess. Then out the door, and back a minute or so later, wiping rain from his face and saying that the window on the passenger side had been down, but he had raised it. The others were closed.

She smiled and said, "Thank you."

"I explained to the hostess that I was only leaving to check the windows."

She said, "Of course. Otherwise she'd have thought you were running out on me."

He said, "I wouldn't do that."

Then something nice happened that added to the pleasure of the evening. From the lounge came the sounds of music. A piano. A few bars of someone warming up, then Cole Porter's "Night and Day."

"How nice, I love music with dinner."

He said that he did, too.

The pianist was good, fortunately. The happy, creative style of a musician enjoying the chance to entertain. Not just someone hired to play for two or three hours.

The next piece was "What is This Thing Called Love."

Apparently the pianist liked Cole Porter.

"Do you come here often, Olney?"

He said, "Not much anymore. I used to bring my wife here a lot. She enjoyed eating out."

He said, "Not that she wasn't a good cook. She was good at everything she did." And was quiet for a moment.

"If anything had happened to me, she could have taken over the business and run it as well as I had."

That was nice. But she had no interest in hearing about his wife.

To change the subject, she asked about his children in California. Where were they and what did they do.

He began telling about them, then stopped, and started laughing.

He said, "I was just remembering something that makes me laugh when I look back on it, although I didn't think it was funny at the time."

She asked what it was.

"You know what a hot tub is?"

She said that she knew what they were, but had never been in one.

He said that his daughter and her husband owned one. When he was out there last fall visiting them, she insisted he try it. Which he did. The only problem was that in their hot tub you don't wear bathing suits.

He said it wasn't the first time he'd been in the water without a bathing suit.

"But it was the first time I'd been in the water with nothing on and my daughter and her three girls in the water with me."

Poor Olney! She reached out and put her hand on his arm and they laughed together.

She could picture him approaching the tub, brushing some hair across his bald spot, then bravely getting in.

From the lounge came the lilting notes of "I Get A Kick Out Of You."

After they stopped laughing, Olney asked her some questions about herself and what she did, and to her surprise she soon found herself talking as if Olney were some old friend she had known many years ago but hadn't seen for a long time, and there were so many things to talk about. Of her marriage, children, career, hopes and dreams. Of tears and laughter, good times and bad.

After a while the waitress was back to see if everything was all right. They said it was, and that they were enjoying the music. Olney said he had always liked Cole Porter.

Mary looked at Olney. For the first time she realized that all the tension was gone. And all the weariness. She had not felt this relaxed for a long time.

She said, "There is one thing that might be nice, if you don't mind."

The waitress asked what that was.

"A candle would be nice. For coffee and dessert."

In the back of her mind she was aware that this was something Dr. Whorter would have approved of. Every woman, he had said somewhere, looks nicer by candlelight.

"I wonder if the piano player plays anything other than Cole Porter?"

Olney said, "Probably. If there is anything you'd like to hear, I'll go ask."

There wasn't. She was just curious. "Cole Porter is all right with me."

She felt a strange feeling coming over her. It was almost like being young again and suddenly thinking that maybe you are falling in love.

She could hardly believe this was happening.

"I bet you have a dog, haven't you?"

He said he did. That he liked dogs.

"You have a cat?"

"Yes. Two of them. Cats make good friends."

He said dogs do, too.

The waitress was back with a tall white candle in a glass candleholder. She lit the candle, then asked if they'd like coffee and dessert. Which they would.

Mary had coffee and the English biscuits. Olney had coffee and apple pie with cheese.

Of course.

They leaned back, smiled at one another. The way two people do who have had a relaxed and enjoyable meal together.

She was not going to be happy seeing this evening come to an end.

What Dr. Whorter would say was that it was not really necessary for the evening to end. Not by their going their separate ways, anyway.

Going to bed with a man is a good way to break the ice.

Which might be true for some people. But not for her. She would never spend the night with a man she had just met.

An enjoyable drink and dinner is one thing. Trying to make more than that out of a simple chance acquaintance is another.

Olney was looking out the window. He said, "It's raining pretty hard, isn't it?"

"Yes."

You would want to get to know a man a lot better before you even thought of spending a night with him. She was sure of that.

Not that she considered herself old-fashioned. Just practical.

From the other room came the opening bars of "Anything Goes."

Olney said, "I always liked this song."

She said, "Me, too."

Ten

One problem Olney had was that whenever a nice woman asks him a question and obviously hopes to get a certain answer, then that is the answer she will get. And the young hostess at the Sanderston Inn clearly wanted him to say yes. So he was not surprised to hear himself tell her that. Yes. He had come for dinner.

He hadn't. He had intended only to stop at the bar and have two beers and watch a bit of TV, if a ball game was on. He had gone without a beer all day, because his old friend was under doctor's orders not to drink and Olney hadn't taken any beer out in the boat because the old man would have wanted some.

The woman Olney found himself sitting across from seemed nice. And quite attractive. She was wearing a yellow dress with some kind of little blue pattern in it, a small pearl necklace, white belt and white shoes. You could tell right away that she hadn't been out in a boat fishing all day.

He guessed that she was probably a school teacher, so it didn't surprise him later to hear her say she had been a librarian.

Same thing, practically.

After a while he realized that he had spent most of the time talking about himself, so he tried to shut up and let her say something. So he asked, "What do you do when you aren't driving around in bad weather? And what brings you here to the Inn?"

She said she had come to have dinner here because the Inn held good memories for her. She and her husband used to come here years ago. She said it had been different then. Simply a good country restaurant where you got a lot of good food for only a small amount of money. That had been a long time ago, back when they were both students at the university.

"In Amherst?"

She nodded.

"Later, when we were both working and had children we still came here on anniversaries or birthdays. Special occasions of any kind."

She did not, however, enjoy driving in bad weather. If she had known it would be raining this hard, she would not have come here on a night like this.

"Is your husband dead now?"

She said, "Yes."

"Sorry."

Because he had talked so much of his own childhood and family, he encouraged her to do the same.

She had married while still in college, which was unusual in those days. She became a librarian, had three children. Her husband was a pianist and composer. Made a living by teaching. They never had much money.

She had mentioned Amherst, so he assumed that that was where she still lived. Amherst, home of the University of Massachusetts, was near Northampton, where Olney used to live before moving to Stockbridge.

She talked, as he had, of her childhood and how good it had been. Of her father, who used to read the classics aloud to the family at night. And classical music in the background at breakfast in the morning. Of a sister and two brothers, a large house near the university, where her father taught.

"I remember parties with famous people in the music or literary world and talking to them the same as if I were talking to people who lived next door or across the street. I didn't realize at the time that some of them were famous."

She said, "Not that it would have made any difference, I suppose."

From the way it all poured out once she got started, he knew that it had been a while since she had had anyone to talk to like this. She said that only five years ago an aunt had died and left her some money, so she and her husband had gone to Europe for two wonderful weeks. She reeled off the names of places they had visited, of museums and galleries.

She had an interesting face. The chin up just a bit. Sort of reaching out. He liked it. And finally remembered what it reminded him of.

Occasionally, along the banks of the Connecticut River you come across a great blue heron standing near the shore. Head aimed sort of up and out. Alert. Perfectly still. It lets you get only so close, then it takes a small leap into the air and very gracefully, legs tucked under and head forward, sweeps up almost effortlessly at about a thirty-five degree angle. One of the most beautiful sights to be seen along the river.

He wouldn't dare tell her she reminded him of a blue heron rising. She would be offended.

Before her husband died, they had made big plans for trips to Europe. On budget prices, of course.

She had made a trip to England a year ago by herself, but had not enjoyed it.

"It's no pleasure travelling alone," she said.

He understood. He said, "It's the same way with fishing."

Then he asked, "Do you mind if I smoke a cigar? They are small and don't smell bad."

She said it would be all right.

"I usually smoke them only outdoors or in my own house. But I do like them after a meal and coffee."

She said once more that it was all right.

"My father used to smoke cigars."

He finished his coffee. She finished hers.

"Could I buy you one more drink?"

She thought maybe a glass of wine would be nice.

Sometimes she looked at him in a way that made him think that she thought he was trying to pick her up. Or that maybe she was trying to pick *him* up. Both seemed rather improbable.

Or were they? He took a few moments to think about it.

It did not seem likely that this attractive, sophisticated, and cultured woman would be interested in a balding man who drank beer and smoked cigars. But should she give any sign that she might actually be, he would certainly do nothing to discourage her.

It had been a while.

"I told you I was sixty-five," he said. "Is it all right if I ask you how old you are?"

"Sixty-three."

"You look younger than that."

"Thank you."

From the lounge came another Cole Porter number. "I've Got You Under My Skin."

He sat there wondering what should be his next move. Nothing crude, of course. He sipped his beer, took a puff on his cigar, rearranged some hair across the top of his head.

The crazy idea came into his head that what he would really like to do was spend the night with this woman. He wondered if she would go home with him, or take him back to Amherst with her. Either way would be all right with him.

One thing he didn't want was for them to simply get back into their cars and go their separate ways.

He looked at her more closely. This was a warm and very beautiful woman and he wanted to do more than simply sit across the table from her. He wanted to be alone with her and take off that nice yellow dress and hold her and run his hands along her body.

He hadn't felt this way for a long time. Now he had to figure out what to do about it.

She said, "Oh, dear!"

And looked out the window.

"What's the matter?"

"I don't like the looks of that weather."

They looked at it together for a moment. The rain had eased up, but the air was misty and very foggy.

A sudden gust of wind threw a large handful of raindrops at their faces, then swept menacingly off as if intending to spin around and return with even more.

"I'm not sure I want to drive home in this kind of weather."

She was looking at him as if she expected him to do something about it.

He gave that some thought. And looked back at her.

If a nice woman has a problem and expects you to do something about it, then you do something. You have no other choice.

He remembered there were guest rooms upstairs.

He said, "Maybe it isn't as bad outside as it looks." And stood up.

"I'll go out and see what it's like."

He did. He walked to the entrance, stepped outside, and stood for a few moments beneath the awning. The road looked clear. Cars were going by as usual. The wind was dying down. The clouds in the west were thinning.

This was not the kind of news that would please her. So when he went back in to give his report, he altered it slightly.

"It looks bad out there. The fog is pretty heavy."

"Really?"

"And it's still raining."

That did it. She made up her mind. She dug into her pocketbook. Pulled out a wallet.

She said, "I don't like driving in bad weather. I'll stay here tonight and get on my way in the morning."

She didn't look too happy with what she saw in her wallet.

"I can give you money if you need it," Olney said. "I happen to have more with me than I need."

"I can always write a check."

"I'd rather give you the money," Olney said.

He got out two twenties and a ten and put them on the table.

"They may already be filled up, you know. But you might as well go find out."

She put her hand on the money, but didn't take it right away.

She looked into his eyes for a long moment, then asked, "Do you think I should do this?"

He looked into her eyes, patted her hand reassuringly and said he thought she should.

"I stopped at the bank this morning, so I happen to have a lot of cash with me."

"What would you do?"

"If I were you? What I would do is take it. It's a gift. You don't have to return it."

She said, "That wasn't what I meant. I meant that if the weather doesn't get better, then what would *you* do?"

He looked at her and said that he didn't know.

"If the weather gets really bad," he said, "I could always ask you to let me share your room."

She nodded. That was always a possibility.

"Of course, since you were paying for it, then I'd be sharing *your* room."

That was true. Olney nodded to show that he was agreeable to viewing it that way.

"Either way is all right with me."

She still seemed a little unsure.

"We'll say that I'm sharing my room with you, since it's not safe for you to drive home in this kind of weather."

That seemed acceptable. She picked up the bills and went to see if the Inn had a vacancy.

They did have, apparently. Olney could see the desk from where he sat, saw her talking to the man behind the counter, saw him take the money, slide the register book in front of her to sign, saw him give her change from the bills.

This was almost too good to be true.

In just a little while he was going to take that good looking nice librarian, now walking toward him, to a room upstairs and to a big comfortable bed and make love to her.

She gave him back the ten-dollar bill and some change.

"We were lucky. All the rooms had been taken, but there was a last minute cancellation, fortunately."

"Probably because of the weather," Olney said.

She agreed. She said, "Probably someone coming from Boston or Connecticut got a weather report and decided to stay where they were."

That made sense.

She handed him the keys to room 2-2. And they finished their drinks. Sighed contentedly, leaned back for a moment, smiled at one another, then pushed their chairs back and stood up.

Olney, remembering that she had forgotten to turn off her lights in the parking lot, watched to see if she would remember to get her book from the window ledge.

She didn't. She started to walk away without it, and Olney had to remind her to get it.

She said she wasn't surprised that she had forgotten it. She didn't seem to have her mind about her all the time anymore.

They didn't go up to the room right away. As they left the dining room and passed through the lounge, the man playing the piano had just returned from a break and was sitting down at the piano. He smiled at them, started playing. They smiled back.

"Do you want to sit down for a few minutes and hear some songs?"

She thought that a good idea, so they sat and listened to some more Cole Porter. And talked. About the kind of music that was popular when they were young and how much better that music was than the kind of music they have today. How things had changed so much, and were still changing.

"I wish I weren't so forgetful. I do things like leaving my lights on and not remembering to take my book with me."

"I wouldn't worry about it."

"Last week I looked all over the house for my scissors and finally found them in the kitchen in the silverware drawer." She laughed. "Of all places!"

He said, "You simply had your mind on something else when you put them there."

And he told her that about a week ago he had come out of the liquor store in town with a six-pack of beer, had put it on top of the car while he talked to someone, then forgot about it and drove off, with it still on top of the car.

"Everyone was yelling at me and waving. I'd honk and wave back. For three blocks I thought I was the most popular person in town."

The piano player, about fifty years old, was short, heavy, round faced. With a beard, he would have made a delightful Santa Claus. He looked around at everyone while he played, enjoying their enjoyment. He played every song as if it were a fresh gift from the bag of goodies he had brought with him. You could tell that playing the piano was, in his opinion, more fun than anything else anyone could possibly do.

Mary rested her hand on Olney's and leaned her head against his shoulder.

"Tired?"

She said she was.

"Ready to call it a day?"

"I think so."

They got up to leave, and again she forgot the book. He had to remind her.

"Thanks. I think I didn't bother to remember it because I knew you would." And laughed.

He didn't quite hear that, and had to ask her to repeat it. Which she did.

On their way out he said it bothered him that his hearing wasn't as good as it once was.

"My memory is as good as ever," he said, "but I don't hear as well as I used to."

Eleven

The weather for Harry's party was just right. Sunny but not too hot, with a clear blue sky and a slight breeze. Not only was the party a big success, but it brought to the deck a new kind of spirit. A family spirit, almost. From that day on, going onto the deck was like going into the family living room. Quarrels and bickering as well as fun and festivity.

That was exactly the way Olney wanted it to be.

Plenty of hot dogs and hamburgers and potato chips. And Olney had made a lot of potato salad of the kind his mother used to make. Everyone liked it.

Brenda said, "I never thought of you as the kind of man who could make potato salad." Then she said, "And I mean that as a compliment."

"Thanks."

Heather liked it a lot. She said, "You ought to make it more often."

"It's a lot of work."

"I'd help, if you wanted me to."

"Good. I'll teach you how to make it. You can make it any time you want to."

She had that hesitant little smile on her face, as if she weren't really sure he meant it.

He said, "I'll show you tomorrow how to make it, and you can take some down to your grandmother and get her opinion on it."

"All right."

DeeDee was at the party. Ordinarily on Sundays she and Charles would be out sailing on the lake, but today he was playing in a golf tournament at the country club. He had assumed she would follow along and watch, as all the other women friends or wives of the players would do, and was not pleased to know she wouldn't be there.

She said, "I told him I wouldn't think of missing Harry's birthday party."

Harry liked that. He felt the same way. "I wouldn't have missed it myself for anything in the world."

That got a laugh or two.

Cheryl and Olney had another cartoon. Not especially funny, but they had already agreed that when they had a lot more, they would go back and throw out the ones that weren't funny.

The characters were now named Bill and Sue.

This was from an idea Olney had gotten from a newspaper item about a Hollywood actress who had recently divorced her fourth husband.

"My cousin Meryl has been married and divorced four times."

"Her name is Meryl Yetz Best Parker Barton."

"She keeps getting calls from perfect strangers."

(Sue) "Why is that?"

"They think she's a law firm."

Harry had a great time. He took two quarters out of Heather's ear and put them under Cheryl's sketch pad and said they could each have one. But when they looked under the pad the quarters were not there. Heather later found them under her napkin.

Otis and DeeDee and Heather played basketball for a while, then Otis started a contest to see who could make the most foul shots out of five tries. He got everyone into the game, even Olney. To make it fair, he put everyone at different distances from the net. Cheryl was only about four feet away. Otis far in the back, beyond regulation distance.

Olney put up a package of cigars for a prize. But it turned out that Cheryl, from only four feet, sank the most shots. So she was awarded the prize. Then she traded the cigars to Olney for a Coke.

Norman Rockwell could have made a nice painting from all that. All of them lined up to take their turn to shoot. No two alike. A different expression on each face.

Or, maybe even better, a picture of Olney bending down to officially present the prize to the youngest athlete of them all.

Later, everyone but Olney and Harry went for a ride with Otis to see the house he had bought out near the college and would move into in October. They even took Solomon with them, although there was not much room. It helped that Heather left her basketball behind and Cheryl left her sketch pad in Olney's care.

Then they were gone and suddenly it was so quiet on the patio that you could hear the silence. You could hear the sound of no basketball hitting the rim of the net and making that ringing noise. Even the fact that no black dog lay sprawled at anyone's feet immediately caught the eye.

"You got a good place here, Olney." And Harry took a sip of his beer. "It's relaxing."

"Thanks. I like it."

He said, "I'm not sure I'd like it if I were here all by myself. And having the kids come up every day helps."

"Nothing so relaxing as being alone," Harry said. And took another sip of his beer. "Makes you appreciate having people around."

Olney liked that.

"That's a good line."

"Thanks." And he said, "Every salesman has to have a good line."

Into Olney's mind popped the memory of the Chicago airport and the fog and having a few drinks with a man named Tennyson.

"Maybe you should have been a writer," Olney said. "Or a professor."

Harry would never have cared for either occupation. He had never wanted to be anything but a salesman. He had come from a long line of salesmen. His father before him, and his father's father.

"It's an honest way to make a living and you learn a lot."

He said, "Why do you think I got the name 'Harry'?"

Olney didn't know.

"My father had been one of the old-time travelling salesmen, and a good one. Made a lot of money and had a good life. Good family man. Because he wanted his sons to follow in his footsteps, he wanted them to have the kind of names that would automatically be turned into friendly nicknames. The kind that goes along with a big hello and a hearty handshake."

He had been named Harrelson. Which becomes Harry, of course.

"Harry," he said. "Great name for a salesman."

He had a brother names Samuelson. Intended to become either Sam or Sammy. Depending upon the price of the product you're selling.

"Father named my sister Regina."

He said. "A man thinks twice before making improper advances to a girl named Regina."

Olney laughed.

"In high school," Harry said, "the boys were almost afraid to ask her for a date."

Olney had some things to say about names.

"Ebert isn't the easiest name a kid can try to live with," Olney said. "And when you're seven or eight years old and playing cowboys and Indians, it's not easy for the other kids, either."

He said, "It doesn't sound right to say. 'They got me in the shoulder, Ebert.' Or, 'Let's cut them off at the pass, Ebert.' "

Harry liked that.

"We named our children John and Jessie," Olney said. "Both good names."

Harry said that Brenda had always liked her name. Her father had been an army officer and she thinks she was named after some kind of machine gun. She isn't sure."

They both had a long sip of their beer.

"She's writing a novel," Harry said. "And you're in it."

Olney said he knew that.

"I'm going to ask her if she'd mind calling me Wes. Or Hank."

Then he said, "You and Brenda make a good pair. I'm happy about that."

Harry said it wasn't quite as good as it appeared to be.

"It's only a summer thing. She's going back to Westport in October and we likely won't see each other again."

"Sorry about that."

"You needn't be. It wouldn't have lasted much longer anyway."

Harry said, "She was married once. It was a bad experience. She says one bad experience is enough."

Olney didn't want to hear about it.

"She made one really dumb marriage when she was twenty-four. Lasted about three years. Convinced her that there's no such thing as a good marriage."

Olney said, "Everyone to their own opinion. I never try to interfere in other people's affairs."

He took the last sip from his beer and tossed the can into the waste basket.

"I guess I've always been satisfied in just being a good plumber."

"Keeping out of other people's lives," Harry said, "is something a plumber can do. You just go in and do the job that has to be done, then leave the bill and go."

True. That was pretty much the way it had been.

"A salesman has to do a lot of listening," Harry said. "Not because he wants to but because he has to. If you don't listen before you start talking, you will probably say the wrong thing and lose the sale."

Olney said, "Maybe so. I guess I'd not have made a good salesman."

"You'd have made a great salesman," Harry said. "You were a good plumber, you'd have made a great salesman."

"I don't think people like to have other people know about their personal life."

"You may be right," Harry said. "But that's not been my experience."

He said, "Lots of times I'm talking with someone and trying desperately to think of some way to get him off the subject he is on, and onto the subject of how much that person really needs this new air-conditioning system I want to sell him. But first I have to listen to them talk about their problems. Business, politics, kids, college expenses, and occasional constipation. And if you've got the patience, they'll tell you about the good time they had at the business meeting in St. Louis last summer, or the time they caught their wife in bed with their next door neighbor."

He said, "You have to listen a lot. But you learn a lot, too."

Otis's car came up the driveway, came to a stop. Doors opened.

Harry said, "I think I'll have another beer. Can I get you one?"

"Thanks."

Everyone said they liked Otis's new house. Heather especially. She said it had a garage, and Otis was going to put up a basketball backboard and net as soon as he moved in.

On the way back, they had passed Charles DeWitt's house, where DeeDee would live when she married Charles. It was big. Four acres of land, five bedrooms, big terrace in back, swimming pool. No other houses very close.

Heather said that at Otis's place there were houses on both sides. She liked that better.

Otis asked Olney if he planned to use the rowboat later. If not, he said he thought maybe DeeDee and he would go out in it for a while. Get cooled off.

Olney told him he could use it, of course. But just as he said that, DeeDee let out a little yelp.

"What's the matter?"

"Oh God! I forgot."

"Forgot what?"

"I was supposed to meet Charles at the clubhouse at five o'clock."

Olney glanced at his watch. It was five-thirty.

"He'll be furious."

Otis said, "Call and say that you will be a little late."

"I can't."

She told Harry how much she had enjoyed his party. Hurried through an apology to Olney for not being able to stay and help clean dishes and things.

Then she looked down at her clothes.

"Do I look all right? Or should I go in and change?"

They all looked at her.

There she stood, possibly the most beautiful young woman in the state of Massachusetts, and she wanted to know if she looked all right.

Well, the shorts did look a bit wrinkled, as if maybe she had been playing basketball or something. And her face was flushed and her hair looked as if the wind had been toying with it. But those things were relatively minor and the total appearance rated an A plus.

Everyone said they thought she looked all right.

Before she left, Harry offered some final advice.

"DeeDee, when you walk into that clubhouse, unless everyone in the room stands up and cheers, turn right around, walk out, and come back here where you're appreciated."

That was a good line. Olney liked that.

Only a salesman could come up with a good line like that.

Olney said, "Bring Charles back with you, if you'd like. There's plenty of beer and more hot dogs."

DeeDee said, "Thanks. But I doubt if he'll come."

The party started drawing to a close. Everyone helped clear away the paper plates and empty cans and bottles and what not. Then Otis went upstairs to finish marking some school papers. Harry and Brenda left. Cheryl and Heather headed for home.

Before they left, Olney said, "If you don't have anything better to do, come on up tomorrow morning."

They said that was what they had already planned to do.

Olney sat on the deck for a while and listened to the chimes in the bell tower. They played "You Are My Sunshine," "Auf Wiedersehen," and "Tomorrow," from the musical *Annie*.

Good songs all of them.

It bothered him to realize that in October Otis would move to his new house, Brenda would be back in Westport, and DeeDee likely either married to Charles or living with him. Which meant that he would have to find three new tenants. And the chances were that he wouldn't be so lucky next time. And if even one of the three proved difficult, the deck wouldn't be fun anymore.

The idea was depressing. He tried not to think about it. He said, "How about Bowker Woods again?"

Solomon stood up. Any place was all right with him.

Twelve

Brenda Sohmner's main source of gossip and inside information in the town of Stockbridge was Lilly DeWitt. Derek DeWitt's sister. Charles's aunt. Brenda was using Lilly not only as a source of information but as a model for one of the characters in the novel she was writing.

Lilly DeWitt has a small but solidly respectable gray and white house on Main Street in Stockbridge, not far from the center of town. Hedges and shrubs and beautiful old shade trees on a gently sloping lot leading to a small stream behind the property that flows into the Housatonic River. Plus a good view of Monument Mountain south on Route 7.

Should you, on any summer day, happen to pass by the house and look through or over the shrubbery, you will see on the side patio a table with a large green umbrella shielding from the sun a gray-haired, thin, seventy-seven-year-old lady. Still attractive, alert, active. About twelve o'clock she will be having a light lunch and a gin and tonic. About one o'clock she will have finished her lunch and will be taking the first sip of her second gin and tonic.

Lilly DeWitt is the oldest of the four children of Willard and Martha DeWitt, and the only one of the four still living in Stockbridge. Her youngest brother, Derek, now fifty-nine years old, grew up in Stockbridge but lives in Manhattan. Both her two other younger brothers left this part of the country years ago. One went to Florida, prospered, and stayed there. The other went to Houston, Texas, and also prospered and stayed. She visited each of them once a year. In the winter months, of course. Both are quite rich, have big houses with swimming pools, expensive cars, and, in Lilly's opinion, an incredibly boring social life.

Not that the social life in Stockbridge is unbearably exciting, but it does have a depth and continuity that is made to order for one such as Lilly, who has for so many years been an intimate part of the upper level of it and an interested observer of what goes on in the lower levels of it.

Brenda Sohmner had met Lilly DeWitt many years ago when she was in Stockbridge researching that first article for *The Atlantic*. She had been only twenty-three years old at the time. Because Lilly had been such a valuable source of information, Brenda had rewarded her by mentioning her name three times in the article. And again in subsequent articles on Rockwell as the years went by.

They would be friends forever.

Brenda could come for lunch and gin and tonics on the patio any time she wanted to.

Brenda, during the summer, had done that at least once a week. Always bringing her pen and notebook. Although both she and Lilly considered the lunch to be simply an enjoyable little social occasion, Brenda thought it best to maintain her role as the young journalist, accepting any information useful to her in reporting on the life and times of Norman Rockwell in the town where he had worked and died.

Lilly had married once, in her early twenties, following a Paris springtime spree, but the marriage had lasted less than two years, and she didn't like to talk about it. He had been her age, a bit less wealthy, and a bit more irresponsible. It had been a fun experience, light and forgettable.

She got the divorce, returned to Stockbridge, resumed her maiden name. And here she stayed, except for an occasional trip to Europe and a month or so in Florida and Houston in the winter.

Her major occupation, she told Brenda, was observing activities and antics of the people here.

She said it was a hobby. Like bird watching.

"And some of the people in this town are real strange birds."

Brenda had written that down the first time she heard it. Now she just laughed lightly and smiled.

Lilly did not care much for the Sedgwicks, one of the old families of Stockbridge. Just why she did not care for them never became clear. Brenda had interviewed members of the Sedgwick family over the years and had found them to be gracious and friendly.

"The DeWitts have been in Berkshire County as long as the Sedgwicks, but the Sedgwicks make more noise about it."

Brenda nodded. Took a sip of her gin and tonic.

"The DeWitts have always been adventurers," Lilly said. "They took off for different parts of the country. Tried different kinds of ways to make money. But the Sedgwicks just stayed here and got older."

That was not a bad line. Brenda has written it down more than once, but she wrote it down still one more time.

She wrote something down every once in a while because she knew Lilly liked to see her do that.

But Brenda had not come here today to make notes. She had come here for a very specific and important reason, which she would get around to as soon as the opportunity presented itself.

"The DeWitts," Lilly said, "are well known all across the United States. They own big companies, have money, and political influence. Power. But the only ones who have heard of the Sedgwicks are the ones who have heard the jokes about the Sedgwick Pie.

"The Sedgwick Pie is the name given to the burial arrangement of the Sedgwick family in the old graveyard in Stockbridge. Judge Theodore Sedgwick, first of the Stockbridge Sedgwicks, and his wife, Pamela, are buried in the center of the large plot under impressive monuments. Their descendants and families, under stones of more modest size, are buried with their feet pointing toward the center. Consequently, when the dead arise on judgment day, the Sedgwicks will stand up facing only the Judge and his wife and other members of the family.

"People heard of Edie Sedgwick, of course. She got the family some publicity. Racing around New York City like a pretty cyclone gone out of control. Died of an overdose of drugs."

On other occasions, in calmer moments, Lilly had grudgingly admitted that the Sedgwicks tended to stay married, avoided unnecessary publicity, were stable and solid.

The DeWitts, Lilly was proud to say, were quite the opposite. They married and had children, if they wished. Got divorced, if they wished. Took their pleasure when and where they found it. Made money in whatever way it amused them to do so.

"Henry Sedgwick's wife was cremated," Lilly said.

"I don't know how they will handle that on the Day of Resurrection when everyone is supposed to stand up and greet everyone else."

Brenda has heard all this before.

She let the old lady talk on, waiting for the right time to bring up the reason why she had come here today and why this nice old lady would have to set aside her pretensions temporarily and deal with a bit of reality.

Lilly had had many lovers. Abroad as well as in Stockbridge.

She now started on that subject. It was one of her favorite topics of conversation.

"Conductors and composers are not good lovers."

Brenda, as always, asked, "Why is that, Lilly?"

"All they think about is their music. Women are never really that important to them."

She told, once again, of a certain lover, whom, as always, she refused to name, who had conducted the Boston Symphony at Tanglewood many years ago. He had the habit of humming to himself as he made love. As he came closer to his climax, according to Lilly, his humming became louder and more spirited.

"His orgasm," she said, "was like a number of short, separate crescendoes."

Brenda laughed, as always.

"Orgasmo Esprito!"

Lilly threw her head back, and laughed. As she always did.

Then, after she stopped laughing and shaking her head, she touched a handkerchief to her mouth and nose, and suggested to Brenda that she fix each of them another drink.

Lilly had nothing good to say about Norman Rockwell. But she had liked his wife, Molly, very much.

"As gracious and charming a woman as you could ever meet. One of the nicest people ever to live in Stockbridge."

Brenda agreed with that opinion. She felt the same way.

Lilly had posed once for Norman Rockwell. He had seen her one Easter morning walking home from church in her very fashionable new dress and stylish wide-brimmed bonnet with bright-colored flowers. He had approached her, identified himself, and had asked if she would pose for him. Which she agreed to do.

A few days later, again dressed in her Easter finery, she posed for the photographer in Rockwell's studio. She was asked to pose holding her right arm down and out at an awkward angle. It was tiring and took a while, but Rockwell had been finally satisfied that he had got the pose he wanted.

The painting became a *Saturday Evening Post* cover.

Two kids were in the painting with her.

The arm she had posed holding down and out was now holding a dog leash, at the end of which was a fancy white poodle strutting along. In the background two roughly dressed boys, holding fishing poles and obviously not on their way to church, were practically in hysterics. They were looking at her Easter outfit, slapping their knees and keeping hands across their mouth to keep from screaming out loud with laughter. Also in the picture was a large mongrel dog, one ear cocked upwards, looking down with bemusement and disbelief at the laughable little poodle.

Lilly had never owned a poodle. She had not even liked poodles. And after she saw the *Post* cover, she didn't like Norman Rockwell.

Brenda was back with the two drinks. Gave one to Lilly, kept one for herself, and sat down again.

"Lilly?"

"Yes, Dear."

"I came here today because there's something I need to tell you."

Lilly crushed a cigarette into the ashtray.

"Then please do."

Brenda hesitated. Lilly reached out and touched her hand. "I suspected all along that you had something on your mind. You've been so quiet."

Brenda said, "Two things, actually."

"All right."

They both took long sips of their drink.

It was pleasant here on the patio, under the large green umbrella. Brenda took a moment to enjoy it. The lovely view, the soft breeze, the feeling of relaxation. This might possibly be her last time here.

"Years ago," she said, "when I was up here interviewing people for my *Atlantic* article, I met your brother, Derek, and accepted his invitation to meet for dinner at his place in New York. Where we would have more time to talk. Over cocktails."

Lilly nodded. "That was nice."

"We ended up having an affair."

"That's even nicer."

She said, "You could have told me that long ago, Brenda, dear. I'm not shocked at things like that."

Brenda said, "I've not yet got to the shocking part, Lilly. I'm building up to that."

"Oh?"

For each of them, another sip of gin and tonic.

"At the same time that Derek and I were starting our affair," Brenda said, "he was bringing another affair to an end. There was no way I could avoid knowing about it."

Lilly raised her eyebrows only the slightest.

"It was an affair he was having with a beautiful young woman from Stockbridge. One whom he had encouraged to come to Manhattan under the pretense that he would be able to help her start a career as a fashion model."

She paused a moment to let that thought sink in.

"It had been a rather cruel affair," Brenda said, "ending in an unwanted pregnancy and the birth of a girl to an unmarried mother."

Lilly said, "Oh, dear." And a moment later, "How unfortunate."

Brenda said, "I'm not passing this along just as another bit of gossip, but because I want to get a burden off my shoulders and on to someone else's."

Lilly asked, "Who would that be?" And smiled again.

"You."

Lilly didn't understand. She finished her drink, set down her glass. And they looked in silence at one another for a long moment.

"Are you ready for it?"

Lilly said, "Of course, dear. What is it?"

"It will shock you."

Lilly reached out and patted Brenda's hand.

She said, "I am long beyond the point of being shocked by anything, Brenda, dear. You just go ahead and say it."

All right.

"The young woman who became pregnant," Brenda said, "was Rhonda Mason. The child she had, she named DeeDee. She took the name from the initials of the child's father. The same DeeDee who is about to become engaged to your nephew, Charles. Her half-brother."

After a moment, she said, "I think you should be the one to tell Charles that DeeDee is his half-sister. Or make Derek tell him."

Another long moment of silence. Lilly just sat there.

Then Brenda did a nice thing. She reached out and took Lilly's glass.

"I've got to go, Lilly. But before I do, let me first get you just one more gin and tonic."

Thirteen

Olney was on the deck reading his morning paper when Heather showed up. She was by herself.

"Where's Cheryl?"

"She can't come up until she finishes cleaning her room."

Heather was an attractive young woman. Dark eyes, full frizzy hair, a soft face and a cautious smile. As if she were not really sure that she was really accepted or welcome. As if maybe someone some time ago had told her that black girls didn't really belong in white company.

There wasn't anything Olney could do about that except hope she outgrew it.

Without the company of her chubby little friend she seemed even a bit more shy, a little less confident. She sat in her chair as if it were not quite as comfortable as usual.

She and Cheryl dressed so much alike that it almost seemed as if they were in uniform. Tennis shoes that once were white, some long time ago, with white socks, frayed blue-jean shorts, and T-shirts.

You could tell that she had something on her mind. So Olney did what he could to help. He leaned back and looked comfortable and relaxed. He said, "Looks like it's going to be a good day."

She thought so, too.

"I hope it doesn't get too hot."

She felt the same way.

"It must get pretty hot out there on that basketball court." Then he put his newspaper aside and added another thought.

"Otis was saying yesterday that you're getting to be a pretty good basketball player."

She liked that. You could tell.

"DeeDee said the same thing."

She liked that, too.

Nothing for a moment. Solomon had sprawled next to her and she patted him and scratched him behind the ears.

"I was thinking the other day," Olney said, "how good it is to see you two kids being such good friends."

He said, "It's been a long time since I was your age, but I still remember how important it is to have at least one special friend you like to buddy around with."

Heather bent down and scratched Solomon's back, then down toward the tail, where he really liked being scratched.

"We may not be together much longer."

He asked why that was.

"Because she's going to run away."

"Really?"

She nodded.

"That's serious."

He unwrapped a cigar. Shook his head a time or two.

"I hope she doesn't."

"Me, too."

He lit the cigar.

"Why does she want to drop out of school?"

"Because all she wants to do is learn how to draw, and she doesn't have to go to school to learn that. And because she and her mother are always arguing."

"What do they argue about?"

"Because all she wants to do is learn to draw."

He nodded. That made sense.

"Incidentally, if you want to help yourself to a Coke, there's some in the cooler."

She said, "I'll wait until Cheryl gets here."

Olney took a puff or two on his cigar, then he said, "I remember how it was when I was a kid. Every summer about this time I'd tell my mother I was going to quit school, and she would say that that was not a bad idea. I was getting too old to go to school, anyway. Almost. Then she'd say maybe I should go to school just one more year, then she thought I should drop out and go to work. That I was getting too big to be in school."

He laughed and blew a puff of smoke in the general direction of Monument Mountain.

"She said that every summer until I finally graduated from high school and went to work."

Solomon raised his head, then got to his feet. Headed down the driveway wagging his tail.

"Don't tell her I said anything."

Olney said, "Of course not. This was just between you and me."

She reached into the cooler. "If it's all right, I'll take a Coke now."

He said, "You might as well get one for Cheryl. She'll want one."

"All right."

"And you might as well get me one, too. Please. It's a little too early for a beer."

"All right."

The day got off to its usual start. Cokes and idle conversation, then Heather to the court to practice jump shots and layups, while Cheryl and Olney started working on their cartoons.

First, Olney mentioned something.

"You remember I said that back when I was in the fourth or fifth grade there was a girl who held her pencil the way you do when you draw?"

She remembered his saying something about that.

"I told you I didn't remember her name?"

All right.

"Well, I finally remembered it. It was Thelma."

He said, "Her name just popped into my mind last night. For some reason."

She said, "Olney, you're funny."

He said, "Maybe so. But her name was Thelma. I remember that."

Olney said he had a couple ideas for cartoons.

One was about a woman who tended to forget things.

The same drawings, of course. Her grandmother, Olney, the can of beer, cigar smoke spiraling upwards.

"Aunt Mildred said she saw her doctor yesterday."

"She asked about her problem of forgetting things."

(Sue) "What did the doctor tell her?"

"She doesn't remember."

Another was from an advertisement he had seen about a doctor treating his patients by hypnosis.

"My sister is going to a hypnotist tomorrow."

"He's going to cure her of insomnia."

"She asked what to do to prepare for the visit."

(Sue) "What did he say?"

"He said relax your mind. And get a good night's sleep."

Because Charles lately had been spending more time in New York on business, DeeDee was home more. She and

Otis and Heather spent more time on the court together playing basketball.

They had progressed to the point where Otis was giving instructions on the more technical aspects of the game. Rules and regulations. When a foul was called and why. Goal tending, travelling, blocking. That kind of thing. How to get your opponent to foul you by getting your feet set before he or she charges into you. Then calling the referee's attention to it by very dramatically falling down and appearing to be hurt.

To show how it was done, when one of them was charging toward the net, he would set himself and then let DeeDee or Heather charge into him and knock him down. He would go flying, fall, roll over, grab onto a shoulder or knee, and put a look of pain on his face. It looked to Olney like a lot of punishment, but Otis didn't seem to mind. DeeDee always helped him up, brushed him off, and apologized. Asked if he were all right.

Olney heard his phone ringing, got up and went inside to answer it.

It was some woman from a real estate office in Great Barrington. She said there was someone who was interested in buying his property and she wanted to know how much he was asking for it.

He told her he wasn't asking anything for it. That it was his home and he didn't plan to sell it.

She understood. But would he please let her come around and see it anyway?

She was new in the real estate business. She had to see people's houses if ever she were to learn about property values.

What could he say? If a woman asks you to do her a favor, you don't say no.

"You can look at the house, but I don't plan to sell it."

"Would tomorrow night at seven be all right?"

He said he supposed so. He'd be here.

They said good-bye, and he went back to the patio.

And got there to find things had changed considerably during his absence. The basketball court was empty. Everyone was sitting down. Otis and DeeDee were arguing over something.

Olney came in at the point where it seemed that the major disagreement was whether or not Otis had ever really been poor. And whether DeeDee had every really been poor or had merely been told she was. The volume level indicated that this was more than a casual little philosophical discussion about life in today's troubled world and what should be considered the acceptable poverty level.

Heather sat off to one side, practicing spinning a basketball on the end of the index finger. She had seen it done on television. Otis had showed her how to do it.

Olney took a chair next to Heather.

"What's the argument about?"

She succinctly described the situation in the minimum number of words.

"Otis doesn't think DeeDee should marry Charles."

She gave the basketball a spin. It fell into her lap.

DeeDee said, "What do you mean, people told me I was poor? I didn't need anyone to tell me I was poor. All I had to do was look at the clothes I wore. See other kids going places I couldn't afford to go to. Have things I couldn't afford to have."

She said, "Being poor is an experience you've never known. That's why you don't know what you are talking about."

He said, "I was poor in a different way. My parents were the town radicals. They didn't have a lot of friends. I was accepted around town only because I could play ball."

"You went to college. You knew all the time you would go to college."

"My father lost his job in the public school because people thought he was a socialist or something."

She said, "At least your father made a living. Had some kind of income. Only two kids and money in the bank, probably. My stepfather had four kids, worked in the mill, was laid off most of the time, couldn't support his family and finally just disappeared."

Otis said, "The only way I got to college was on an athletic scholarship. And I had to work to help pay my way."

She said, "Big deal."

"What I'm trying to get you to see is that there were kids who tried to make me feel inferior because their family belonged to the country club and mine didn't. And people tried to make you feel poor because you didn't have fancy clothes. It's the same thing."

She responded to that in a low and patient tone of voice.

"There is no comparison, Otis, between not getting to go to the big dance at the country club and not going to the high school junior prom because you don't have anything decent to wear."

"You could go to Berkshire Community College if you wanted to. I could get you in."

"And work nights to pay for it? When everyone else was home studying or out dancing?"

After a moment, she said, "And you're damn right I'm interested in his money. Which is what you said that got all this started."

She said, "I can hardly wait to get my hands on some of it. I can think of lots of things I'd like to buy with it."

Otis was not winning this argument. You could tell that.

She said, "There are some people besides myself I plan to spend some of it on."

Heather asked Olney if he'd like to go throw a few.

"All right."

Anything to get away from this argument.

"Besides, I'm not marrying the man just for his money. It so happens that he also is good looking, educated, polite, well mannered. Things like that. We have fun together. Sailing. Dancing. You name it."

"You'll be miserable."

On the way to the court Olney suddenly realized Cheryl was missing.

"Where's Cheryl?"

"She went home." Heather took a shot from far out and missed.

"She doesn't like to hear people arguing."

Olney said, "Me, either."

He tried to keep his elbow in when he shot. It wasn't easy.

She retrieved the ball and handed it to him.

"And try to follow through more."

He tried that. Missed again. Then he retrieved the ball, handed it to her, admitted that he'd never made a good basketball player.

He said he was better at fishing.

"I'm going to dig some worms and go out in the boat. If you want to come along, you can."

All right.

"But I want to ask Cheryl if she wants to come with us."

Olney said, "Of course. I'd planned to stop by her house on the way."

He got an empty coffee can and they headed for the garden.

"Don't let me forget the Cokes and beer."

She said she wouldn't.

"Remember to bring along some of your cigars."

He said he wouldn't forget those.

Otis was saying, "I know these people. Their social life is their whole life. Unless you can trace your family back to the American Revolution they'll look down on you."

"I won't be marrying into a social set. I'll be marrying a man who loves me."

"Don't kid yourself. You'll be marrying into a tight little social circle that will slowly strangle you."

"Let them try."

"I've seen them do it."

"Not to me, they won't."

Olney and the kids tried a different fishing spot this time. Down near the causeway. The girls didn't care for his idea of not using bobbers, just using worms on the bottom, but it worked. Cheryl caught two good-sized trout and Heather a sixteen-inch bass.

He cleaned Heather's bass to take home and give to her grandmother.

"If she likes it, tell her you'll catch some more for her."

He cleaned Cheryl's trout, who said she thought maybe she'd save them and take them up to her grandmother in Pittsfield tomorrow.

"If she doesn't want them," Olney said, "she can give them to a neighbor. And if the neighbor doesn't want them, she can give them to her cat."

He said, "She does have a cat, probably."

"Yes."

"Good. And make sure you tell her that you caught them."

He was watching the ball game that night when he got a call from his son, George, just checking to see how Olney was doing. He asked if Olney was keeping busy.

"Not too much. Doing a little fishing. That's about all."

It was George's opinion that Olney would be better off going back to work and keeping active.

"You retired too early," George said. "You're going to sit out there on that patio and after a while lose interest in things. It's unhealthy to retire too early. People who keep active live longer."

George ran several miles every day, plus a number of laps in his swimming pool in his back yard.

Olney admitted he was probably right.

"Someone wants to buy this house," Olney said. "Probably for a lot more than I paid for it. Maybe I'll take the money and go to Florida and buy a fishing boat and take people out on fishing trips."

That was something George himself had suggested once.

"Good idea."

"You and Vera and the kids can come down and visit and we'll all go out on the boat."

"We'd like that."

Then Olney asked about Vera and the kids and they came to the phone, one at a time, to tell him how great California was and about the new station wagon they'd bought. Things like that.

They all said they hoped Olney would come out for another visit soon, and he promised he would. Maybe this fall.

The real estate lady came around the next night at seven. She was about forty, stout, wore a pants suit, a dumb floppy blue hat, knew more about property values in town than she had admitted to on the phone. And didn't like dogs. She said she was afraid of them. She wanted Olney to tie up Solomon, which he refused to do.

She said, "I don't want him to jump up on me."

"He won't jump up on you," Olney said. "I'm not sure he even likes you."

He showed her around the property through the apartment, which she thought smelled of cigar smoke and needed redecorating. She also told him he wasn't handling the property properly. What he should do was rent the apartments for high rates during the Tanglewood season, then at regular rates during the other months. He would make much more money that way.

He didn't like that idea at all.

But he was impressed by the amount of money she said her client was willing to pay.

"You sure he wants to pay that much?"

"He doesn't want to. But he's willing to. If I tell him he can't get it for less."

It was more than he had expected. But he said he wouldn't take it. He liked it here.

She left her business card anyway, in case he changed his mind.

Fourteen

What Mary Ostrowski was thinking that night as she walked upstairs to their room was "Don't think about it." This was not a moment of decision. This was simply the continuation of a decision she had made earlier. She did not want to go back out into that weather and she did want to spend the night with this really nice man she had met. She had no reason to feel apprehensive. He was someone she liked and felt comfortable with. What she was doing was right. Dr. Whorter certainly would have approved.

Besides, if it turned out that neither of them felt really comfortable about going to bed together, having met only a few hours ago, they could simply laugh about it, talk about it, and sleep in separate beds. And in the morning have breakfast together and arrange to meet soon for dinner and dancing. Maybe tomorrow night.

That comfortable feeling was shattered almost immediately.

He unlocked the door, held it open for her, and she walked into the room. She heard the door shut solidly behind her, felt reality raise its ever-present head and almost panicked.

He did something he shouldn't have done. He turned her around, pulled her to him, kissed her harder than he should have, ran a hand down her side and to her rear, hugged her too hard and too long before releasing her.

(She later told him that what he had done had frightened her, and he apologized.)

He pulled away, finally, gave her the big comforting smile that she liked, moved in to look at the room. and she followed.

There were two large beds, a thick brown carpet, wood paneling, mirrors, bath and shower. Pretty much what you would expect. Except that here the decor was maybe a bit softer and more country-comfortable. Rustic, almost. The kind of room that would be relaxing to the most apprehensive bride, to the uneasy couple on an extra-marital rendezvous, or two older romantics who had not made love to anyone for a while.

She moved to the window. The view from room 2-2 was exactly as it had been from their table in the dining room, except from one story higher. The brook and the woods behind it. You could see the road from here, if you leaned forward and looked to the left. And you could hear the muffled sounds of cars and trucks. She liked that. This was not isolation, just a warm and comfortable haven from the weather. Still part of the real world.

She said, "I like the room. Do you?"

"Looks good to me."

She looked toward the window.

"It's certainly better than being out on the road on a night like this."

He agreed with that.

There was a large color TV set, but he hadn't given it a glance. He was obviously not about to suggest they might turn it on and see if maybe there was an old movie they might enjoy. Or the news, or a ball game.

He was sitting in one of the chairs and taking his shoes off.

She said, "I never did enjoy driving in the rain."

He said, "I'd rather be here with you anyway, even if it weren't raining."

She liked that. That was a nice thing to say.

He sat there looking at her, the big smile on his face, quite happy at being where he was.

He took off his shirt. Then his trousers.

She remembered some things Dr. Whorter had said.

Don't expect the older widower to come rushing at you with heavy breathing and passionate speech. After many years of marriage he no doubt became accustomed to simply tossing the covers back, sitting on the edge of the bed, then sort of throwing his legs up and falling down on his back. At the same time giving a small satisfied groan and some comment about how good it feels to get to bed.

(Not that it is important, but Dr. Whorter also said that women ususally climb into bed front side first, and lie for a few moments on their stomach.)

Instead of heavy breathing, passionate words, eager hands pawing at you, he will at first likely do little more than say how nice you look. That you have nice breasts. Or thighs. Or something.

Occasionally, not too often, maybe there will be a glass of wine and some soft music.

Mary sat on the edge of the bed and started taking off her shoes. Then stopped and looked at him.

"I wish now I'd suggested that we have them send up a bottle of wine."

She realized immediately that she should not have said that.

He put his shirt back on, then his trousers and shoes.

He said, "What kind of wine would you like?"

She said that any kind would be all right. But that he really didn't need to go for it.

"We can do without it." She said, "I'm sorry I even mentioned it."

By that time he was on his way to the door.

He said, "I'll be right back."

All right.

Mary undressed, put her clothes on a chair, decided she would take the side of the bed near the window. It would be nice to wake up and look out at the brook and trees. Maybe hear the birds singing. Then went into the bathroom and spent a few awful moments looking into the mirror and feeling sorry for herself.

She would win no beauty contests with legs like that. And the breasts were too small, the wrinkles too many. The hips too broad. And the face looked tired.

But she worked as best she could with what she had. Washed her face, brushed her teeth as well as one can do when they don't have a toothbrush, spent a long moment wondering if she should put on a little perfume.

Decided against it.

She found a mint in her bag, popped it into her mouth. Found some more, put them on the table beside the bed. Then got into bed just as Olney, the big smile still on his face, came in with the wine and two wine glasses.

She could picture how it must have looked downstairs a few minutes ago. The big man, grinning, walking into the bar, asked for a bottle of wine. Any kind of wine. And two glasses. Then hurrying back toward his room upstairs.

"That was really nice of you, Olney."

He said, "I just thought of something else I should have done while I was down there."

"What was that?"

"I should have got you something you might want to eat. Nuts or cheese and crackers, or something."

She had sense enough to keep her mouth shut.

"Should I pour you some wine now, or do you want to wait 'til I come to bed?"

"I'll wait until you come to bed."

"All right." And he headed for the bathroom.

"I'll be right back."

Before he closed the door behind him, she called to him.

"Watch out for the mirror. I think it's broken."

She heard him going to the bathroom, flushing the toilet, washing his face and rinsing his mouth. Then he was back.

"I didn't hear what you said as I went into the bathroom."

"I said to watch out for the mirror. It's broken. It makes people look much older than they really are."

He liked that. And laughed.

Which pleased her. It's always good to have someone appreciate a good line when you happen to think of one.

He said, "Don't pay any attention to what mirrors say."

He said, "You look good to me." And he took off his clothes again, and tossed them on the chair on his side of the bed.

He looked pretty good. Legs maybe a bit too thin for the rest of the body. And even though he was holding his stomach in, he was thick around the waist and chest.

She watched as he opened the wine. He poured two glasses full, almost to overflowing, handed one to her. Then put the bottle and his glass on the table next to him.

Then he threw the covers back, sat for a moment on the edge of the bed, and, as she anticipated, threw his legs up and then fell down softly on his back with a small satisfied groan.

He said, "Bed feels good."

Then he rolled over and sat up. He got his glass of wine from the table, turned and faced her.

She raised her glass and touched it to his.

"Here's to us. I think we broke the ice."

You could tell that he wasn't sure what she meant. But he agreed, anyway.

"I think so, too."

They each took a sip of wine.

It was then that she told him how he had scared her when they first came into the room by grabbing her too quickly and holding her too hard.

He said, "Sorry. I didn't mean to scare you."

They touched glasses again.

She looked at him, lying there naked. And suddenly started laughing.

His smile disappeared. He brushed some hair across the top of his head, and asked what she was laughing about.

She said, "I was remembering your story about visiting your daughter in California and having to get into the hot tub with her and her teenage daughters. And none of you with any clothes on."

She said, "That's a funny story."

The grin returned. He laughed, brushed some hair across his head once more.

He said, "I was really embarrassed."

Dr. Whorter said that the first night in bed with a partner after having been sleeping alone for a long time will be easier than you might think.

It will all come back to you. It's like riding a bicycle. Once you've learned how to do it, you never forget. You may not have ridden a bicycle for years, but someone put a bicycle in your hands and within minutes you will be as comfortable and confident with it as if you have never been without it.

Don't feel you need to rush things. Take it slow and easy. It may be that for a while you will want to just lie there and talk.

Olney pulled the covers down all the way so he could see her body full length.

"You look nice."

All right.

She said, "You do, too."

He put his glass of wine on the table.

She said, "Let's just lie here for a while and talk."

You could tell that he didn't care much for that idea. He began running his hands along her body.

"You have nice breasts."

She was tempted to reach down and pull the covers back up. But he would simply have pushed them back down again.

He bent over and kissed her breasts. Took the nipples into his mouth and sucked gently on them.

She put the wine on the table next to her before she spilled it.

He put his mouth hard on hers and kissed her and at the same time ran a hand along her thighs.

Now she found herself being moved into a realm of feeling she had not known for a long time. Physical desires that she had consciously kept under control suddenly broke free. Her body became a thing with a mind of its own, making strong demands for attention.

Here, it said, is where I want to be touched and rubbed. And touched and rubbed there, too. And over there. And here. And back here some more.

He now had his hand where no hand had been for a long time. And it felt good. She responded. She ran her hands along his body everywhere, moved her body in small ways to show that she was ready.

He was bulky and heavy but not crushing. Everything else in the world was blocked out. The feeling she had was that of being most happily overwhelmed by something she had asked for and had no wish to resist. Any pretense at resisting only added to the enjoyment.

He said, "Am I hurting you?"

158

She said, "No. Please don't stop."
He didn't. He kept on.
She said, "Oh, Lord!"
It was so good.
She said, "Oh, God!"

Fifteen

Olney woke up to the sound of the shower running. It took him a few moments to realize where he was, then a little longer to remember how he had got here. Then, having remembered, he smiled, stretched out beneath the covers and felt good about everything.

Hard to believe it had really happened. But it had. Fate. So nice when it works in your favor. Everyone deserves to have something nice happen to them every once in a while.

He could see that the sun was shining. Sunlight covered the part of the bed where she had been. The side nearest the window. Which was probably what had awakened her.

Sun in her eyes.

The sound of the shower ended and he heard the miscellaneous bathroom noises, plus small mumblings and muffled snorting of a person communicating to herself and about life in general, and early mornings in particular.

She came out, undressed, drying herself, looking a bit older in the bright daylight than she had looked last night. But still really nice. He looked at her and admired what he saw.

She gave him a nice smile.

"I see you finally woke up."

He watched as she put one foot on the bed to balance herself as she dried her toes. At age sixty-three you don't try to stand on one leg, like a stork, and dry the other leg.

It is nice to hear a human voice first thing in the morning. Especially a nice friendly voice. It had been a while since he had had that experience.

"Yes, finally."

He watched her nice body as it moved, and remembered how good it had felt last night.

She said, "I pushed you a few times to see if you were still alive. I was pretty sure you were, because you rolled over and went back to sleep."

A good line. He liked that.

"Did I snore?"

"Only a little. Not too bad." She said, "A sort of low rumble. Like distant thunder."

Olney said, "I did that on purpose. I was afraid that if you thought the storm had ended, you'd get out of bed and get in your car and leave."

She said, "That idea would never have occurred to me."

She finished drying her feet, then ran the towel again across certain parts and areas of her body that he had himself rubbed so happily only hours ago.

"Sun wake you up?"

"Yes." Then she draped the towel around her shoulders and walked to the window and looked out.

"It's a beautiful day."

"Good."

The sun shining on her bare body gave it a nice glow. With shadows.

"You look kind of beautiful yourself."

"Thank you." She said, "It's a nice morning and I feel good."

He said, "You felt good last night, too."

All right. She laughed.

"I enjoyed making love to you last night."

She said, "I enjoyed it, too."

She looked out the window again, up toward the tops of the trees and the sky, and seemed pleased with what she saw.

Olney was looking at the soft and well-rounded buttocks, framed in sun and shadow, seeing there something that touched him deeply but could be put aside for some other time. Something about maturity and fullness and womanhood.

He said, "You know what I'd like?"

She did. You could tell. She tossed the towel on the chair and climbed back into bed. She got in front first, lay for a moment on her stomach and looked at him.

He said, "You smell good."

"Thanks."

Making love to her this morning was different. Better. Last night the eagerness to get inside the body of that nice woman had been overwhelming. Nothing else had really mattered. Probably any man who had been a long time without a woman would have felt the same. There is a tension that has built up that demands satisfaction.

Nothing wrong with that.

He said, "I'm glad you said you enjoyed making love last night."

"I did. Or I wouldn't have said so."

That was nice. He believed her. You could look into her eyes and tell.

They were nice eyes and this morning he took more time to look into them. A sort of grayish blue. Soft. Restful.

"You have nice eyes."

"Thanks."

This morning he was willing to just lie there and talk for a while before making love, but most of the talk was about that one thing, how good she looked and felt and was. They spent more time kissing this morning and he thought how good it would be to spend the first minutes every morning just lying there breathing in her breath, looking at her eyes.

He moved her onto her back and pulled her into the middle of the bed.

She said, "Go a little easy. I'm a bit sore."

This nice woman last night had been only a nice woman who looked good and was going to go to bed with him and let him make love to her. Which in itself is pretty good and almost enough.

But there is more, and this morning Olney knew what it was.

He liked this woman. He really liked her very much. He loved her. He loved her. He loved her very much. And the rhythm of it matched the rhythm of the way their bodies moved together until he said it aloud, said it aloud, said, "I love you," said it twice, then again once more just before all the tension built up to that inevitable moment when his long heavy sound almost drowned out her small excited one, and he collapsed upon her, but lightly. And rested.

Later, he brushed some hair away from her face. Kissed her.

"Thank you, Olney. That was nice."

While he had his shower, Mary stayed in bed and felt happy. Heard birds singing outside, saw the sun get even brighter.

She watched him come into the room, put one leg up on the bed to balance himself while he dried his toes.

She said, "Don't worry about it, but you talk to yourself in the shower."

"Do I?"

She nodded.

"But don't worry about it. Everyone who lives alone very long does it."

She made up a statistic appropriate for the occasion.

"Eighty-seven percent of those people over fifty-five who live alone for more than one year talk to themselves in the shower."

Dr. Whorter had said in his book that after an older woman finally resumed her sex life after having gone without sex for awhile, she always has one or the other of two strong feelings about it.

There will be, of course, that real exhilaration that comes from happily doing something that she had for so long felt apprehensive about doing. This may lead to the feeling that now a whole new world of even greater and more enjoyable sensual pleasures lay in store for her. Even more or better sexual partners to be found.

On the other hand, she may be so relieved at having finally found a sexual partner again that she will want to hang on to him desperately because she fears that should she let him get away, she may never find another. She does not want again to go into that long period of searching.

Dr. Whorter's advice was this. Relax.

If you want to see the man again, you no doubt will be able to do so. And if you don't want to see him again, you don't have to. You will have no trouble finding another. Now that you have broken the ice.

Mary lay there, stretched herself across the bed, and relaxed.

Olney went over and sat on the edge of the bed and looked down at that nice woman lying there under the covers and smiling.

She said, "I'm happy about being here. Olney. Are you?"

"Of course." And bent down and kissed her.

"But you can't just lie there in bed all day."

She said, "Why not?"

Why not?

He thought about that. Couldn't think of a good answer.

He tossed his towel on the floor and got back into bed.

The inn didn't serve breakfast. With only three guest rooms, it didn't pay to open up the kitchen in the morning. But one of the workers in the kitchen offered to get them coffee. They could drink it at the bar or take it outside to one of the picnic tables.

They preferred a picnic table. Olney said he'd bring the coffee out, so she went ahead and selected a table near the brook. She had her book—this time she had remembered all by herself to take it with her when she left the room—and put it on the seat.

She walked over to the edge of the brook, swollen by last night's rain, and watched the water sparkle and dance its noisy tumbling way downstream. Watched the squirrels scampering along the ground and the birds making swift flights from one tree to another, and revelled at the thought of being part of it all.

It was a morning for feeling good about everything.

Olney came out carrying two cups of coffee, which he put on one of the tables. Not the one she had selected a minute ago, but all right. One was as good as another. She went to join him.

"Isn't the brook lovely?"

He nodded, walked to the edge of it, then went slowly a dozen yards or more upstream, looking intently into certain parts of it. Turned and came back.

"I guess I will never be able to walk along any kind of water without looking to see if there are any fish in it."

He asked if she had done much fishing and she said that she hadn't. But she loved to be on the water or in the woods. She loved nature. The beauty and poetry of it.

They went back to the table.

"I remembered from last night that you had your coffee with cream but no sugar."

"Right. Thank you."

She said, "I hope you noticed that I remembered all by myself to bring my book when I left the room."

He said that he had noticed. Then for a while didn't say anything, just sort of stared into his coffee, thinking. He was either tired or feeling the letdown from the high of last night and this morning. Maybe after a while she would feel the same way.

But not yet.

She watched a sharp-edged white cloud sail across the tip of a tall pine tree. Then looked again at the brook and into the woods. Sipped her coffee. And suddenly remembered something from a long time ago. The kind of memory that comes flying unannounced and unrequested out of the past.

She said it out loud.

"I sing of brooks, of blossoms, birds and bowers,
Of April, May, of June and July-flowers."

He looked pensively at her across the top of his coffee.

"That's something I suddenly remembered from a poem my father used to read to us years ago. I don't recall the rest of the poem or even who wrote it."

She said, "Whenever he could get us kids together long enough to sit still and be quiet, he'd read us some poetry."

He smiled, but didn't say anything.

"It was his way of making sure we grew up to appreciate the best things in life."

She said, "I think I mentioned that last night at dinner."

He didn't say anything.

"Do you like poetry?"

"Some."

He looked out toward the brook again.

"I guess I was mostly just a plumber."

She asked if his father had ever read poetry out loud to the family, and he said he hadn't.

"Mostly he had just got off work and was tired. Or if he wasn't working he was fixing the fence or repairing the shed."

He took a sip of his coffee.

"I doubt if the old man knew any poetry."

He said, "He knew a lot of other things. But I don't think he knew any poetry."

She said, "We had so much poetry around our house that it was coming out of our ears. As well as going into them."

It all seemed not really very long ago. She could almost see it again. Hear the music. See the faces.

"They were always having parties with honored guests who were either brilliant writers or composers. Artists, sometimes. And we were always supposed to be on our good behavior. Be polite. Go to bed early."

She saw him light one of his little cigars.

"I remember a poem my father liked and used to read to us a lot. Especially when he got older."

"A nice little poem."

"I strove with none; for none was worth my strife.
Nature I loved, and next to Nature, Art;
I warmed both hands before the fire of life;
It sinks, and I am ready to depart."

She said, "Whenever I hear that poem or read it, I think of him."

"Did he write it?"

She said he hadn't. "It's an old poem. Written a long time ago."

He finished his coffee.

"Did you like it?"

He said he supposed it was all right. If she thought it was a good poem and liked it, then he was glad.

She had the feeling that maybe she had made a mistake talking about poetry. He had said last night that neither of his parents had gone beyond the eighth grade, and that he hadn't cared much for high school except for sports.

"It's simply a nice little four-line poem that an old man wrote for himself on his seventy-fifth birthday. About how he had enjoyed life to its fullest, enjoying nature and art especially, and how having lived with all his heart and soul, he saw his life coming to an end and was ready to go."

She said, "It's not important. I'm sorry I mentioned it."

"We all feel that way," Olney said. "Even if we aren't poets."

She agreed with that.

"Of course. It's just that he expressed the feeling in a more beautiful way than most of us could have done." Then she added, "But let's not talk about poetry."

She saw him brush some strands of hair across his head.

"Nature the man loved. Then art." He said, "What was third? People?"

All right. So she shouldn't have brought poetry into the conversation. She should have known better.

On the other hand—and she suddenly felt the strong need to hold her ground—you shouldn't simply be silent about things that are important to you. Two grown people aren't ever going to have exactly the same opinions about everything.

"He never strove with anyone? Does that mean that he was born rich?"

She said, "It's only a poem, Olney. Some people are poets and some aren't." She said, "I'm not. But I like poetry. And I happened to like that particular poem."

"I couldn't say that I never strove with anyone."

He said, "I strove all the way up a beach in Italy just to get back to my wife and kid."

All right.

"I remember lots of times in high school when I got a football handed to me and I strove like hell to get all the way to the other end of the field. And a lot of people strove to stop me."

He said, "I can think of lots of other times, too, when I strove to do something that really needed doing."

She said, "Olney, all the old man meant was that he thought there were things in life more important than human strife. Things like nature and art. Or making love. Or drinking beer and fishing. What he didn't like was strife with people about things that weren't important."

He said, "I had an older brother who flew a P-51 during the war and strove to get back to his home field after a mission and was shot down before he made it."

She said, "I'm sorry, Olney. I had nothing to do with that. Neither did the old man who wrote the poem."

"I should have learned more about nature and art," Olney said. "I know that. But I didn't. In our family we became things like plumbers, contractors, truck drivers."

She shook her head. "You're too sensitive, Olney." She said, "You're taking it too seriously."

"My wife was pretty much the same as I was."

He said, "Between the two of us, probably we couldn't name a dozen poets or painters. Or know one opera star from another. But together we could take a pump apart and put it back together again. And there were times I was short of help and she'd come help me out in some cold wet basement if I needed her to."

There is only so much you can take. This was too much. She had no interest in his wife or pumps or what they did in cold wet basements.

"That's nice, Olney. I'm glad she could do those things. Those are things I couldn't do. Wouldn't care to do."

She said, "We're all different. My husband probably didn't even understand how a pump works. I know that I don't."

She finished her coffee. Looked into the woods and back to the brook and a little ways upstream.

"Paul was a musician. And composer. He played the piano so beautifully that it was almost more than I could stand. A Beethoven sonata so rich and full that it could send your mind and soul out of sight."

She said, "That was part of the reason why I loved him."

But it was now she who was saying the wrong things. She looked down at her empty cup. Pushed it a few inches away from her.

"Beethoven?"

She didn't say anything.

"I've heard of Beethoven. He's dead, isn't he?"

Of course he's dead. For God's sake.

Any man with a brain in his head knows he's dead.

"So's Lou Gehrig!"

That did it. He threw his head back and laughed.

She did, too. And suddenly all the tension was gone.

"That was a good line." He laughed again. "I liked that."

She said "Thank you. I thought it was pretty good myself."

Olney reached out and covered her hand with his. Bent over and kissed her on the mouth.

"I'm sorry."

She said, "Me, too." Then she said that if he would like another cup of coffee, it was her turn to get it.

He said that he didn't want another cup of coffee, himself, but if she wanted one he'd go get it for her.

But what he would prefer was that they go get some breakfast. "Do you know a good place nearby where we can get something to eat?"

Because she assumed he still lived in Northampton, she tried to think of a place that would not take him too far from there. But nothing came to mind. She told him that.

A man had come out of the side door of the inn and was standing there, lighting a cigarette.

Olney said, "Wait here. I'll go ask that man if he knows of a place."

"All right."

But he didn't get up right away. There was something he wanted to say first.

"I hope you know how much I enjoyed our night together."

"Thank you. I enjoyed it, too."

He said, "I don't mean just the night in bed."

He said, "I mean *you*. I mean spending the night with *you*."

She nodded. "I know what you mean, Olney."

He touched her lightly on the arm, then stood up.

"I'll be right back."

From where she sat, Mary could hear only part of the conversation. She saw the man point toward the road, then to the right, then right again. Then left.

Olney thanked him, started back toward her, then turned and asked once more the name of the place. The man answered. Olney said thanks, came back and sat down.

"There's a place about two miles from here. A small place that sells gas, and groceries. There's a small luncheonette with tables inside and, in good weather like today, tables out in back. The man said the food was good."

That was perfect. Just what she wanted.

"If you want something fancier, we'll have to go back to Route 20."

"As long as they serve breakfast, it will be fine with me."

All right.

So he gave her directions.

"Go out to the road and turn right. Almost right away, no more than a few hundred yards, you come to Highland Road."

She nodded.

"Turn right. Go half a mile. Turn left on Toureen Road."

She nodded again.

"Another half a mile and you'll see a place called Smiley's."

"Smiley's?"

"Smiley's. Smiley's gas station or food store. Or something."

He said, "Anyway, why don't you just follow me."

That was a good idea. She said she'd just follow him.

"You lead the way." And they both stood up.

Olney took the coffee cups back to the kitchen, thanked the people there, walked to the parking lot.

He got into his car. Saw her getting into hers.

It was at that moment it first occurred to him she might not follow him. That she might just continue happily on her way. That feeling grew stronger, and by the time he got through the parking lot and up to the road, he felt certain of it. She wouldn't follow him.

He had made a fool of himself.

He should have apologized more. He should have said more about how much he had really enjoyed being with her. How much he really wanted to see her again. That he did like poetry and music, but just hadn't learned to appreciate it.

She probably thought he didn't like cats.

He could live with cats, if he had to. And learn to like them.

He saw her car finally begin to move.

He pulled onto the road, turned right, watched for her in the rear view mirror. Didn't see her. Saw two cars get behind him before he got to Highland Road and turned right.

After he made the turn, he pulled off to the side of the road, then walked back to the intersection to see if she were coming.

He was sure by this time that she wasn't going to follow him.

And he was right. She didn't.

He saw her sail slowly by. Looking straight ahead, off toward wherever she was headed. Chin up just the slightest bit, giving her profile that forward look. The great blue heron. It would not have surprised him to see her car take a short hop into the air, then head upwards at about a thirty-five degree angle.

He watched as her car went up and over a small hill and finally passed out of sight.

Sixteen

Olney got back into the car, sat there for a minute or so, debated whether or not to chase after her. He could catch up with her, force her off the road, make her listen to him whether she wanted to or not.

He decided against that. What more could he say? He had already apologized. She had already made her decision. Everyone is entitled to make his or her own decisions.

And she was probably right. Spending a night in bed with a retired plumber was one thing, getting involved is another.

He started the engine, continued on his way. Half a mile farther on he found Toureen Road, turned left, and shortly after that came to the little store with the gas pumps in front. He parked around in back of the building, went over to one of the small tables and sat down.

Anyone but a retired plumber would have had sense enough to at least get a woman's full name and address and phone number before letting her get into her car. All he knew about her was that she was a widow and lived in Amherst.

A waitress came over, said good morning, took his order. She was a nice cheerful buxom blond who would have cheered up anyone who was not at the moment beyond any possible hope of being cheered up. Ever.

He sat there quietly having breakfast, trying not to think of anything at all. He looked at the trees on the hill behind the building, watched young couples having breakfast together, smiled at a young mother getting baby food into the mouth of an active and ever moving child in a high chair. Noticed one table where two young couples were laughing and making a lot of noise. An older couple next to them eating in disapproving silence. Watched a little girl throwing a stick her dog was supposed to go fetch and observed the dog's preference for a different set of rules. One in which the dog got the stick and was supposed to not let the girl get it back.

While Olney sat there trying not to think of anything, he thought of something.

He remembered seeing Mary, walking toward her car in the parking lot, carrying her pocketbook. What she wasn't carrying was her book. The book that Olney had rescued twice before.

He signalled for the waitress.

No, he didn't want a second cup of coffee. He wanted to pay his check.

"I've got to go. I just remembered something."

He left a dollar on the table, got into his car and headed for the inn.

He pulled into the parking lot, got out of his car and walked over to the table where they had had their coffee. Looked for the book and couldn't find it. Which he found hard to believe. It should have been lying right there, next to where she had been sitting.

He finally found it at a table over closer to the brook. How it had got there, he would never know.

By this time the little book looked quite familiar. He sat down on the bench to examine it.

The title of the book was *Sonnets From The Portuguese*. By Elizabeth Barrett Browning.

He opened it and read one of the poems.

If thou must love me, let it be for naught
Except for love's sake only. Do not say
'I love her for her smile . . . her look . . . her way
Of speaking gently, . . . for a trick of thought
That falls in well with mine, and certes brought
A sense of pleasant ease on such a day'—
For these things in themselves, Beloved, may
Be changed, or change for thee,
                        —and love so wrought,
May be unwrought so. Neither love me for
Thine own dear pity's wiping my cheeks dry,
A creature might forget to weep, who bore
Thy comfort long, and lose thy love thereby.
But love me for love's sake, that evermore
Thou may'st love on through love's eternity.

Olney walked over to the inn, found the front door locked. Went around to the side entrance and walked in. No one was at the registration desk, but a woman was working in the bar area, mopping the floor.

She looked up long enough to say, "We're closed. We don't open until one o'clock.

"I just want to leave a message for someone."

She said, "You have to do that in the office. And they don't open until one o'clock."

Olney said, "Maybe I could leave the message with you."

Without interrupting her work, she asked, "What is it?"

He said, "This is very important." And waited.

She finally stopped, leaned the mop against the bar, came over and asked what the message was and who was it for.

He skipped over the part about how he had spent the night with a woman who had taken off without having breakfast with him.

"A woman I was having coffee with this morning left this book on one of the picnic tables outside." And he held up the book so she could see it.

"I'm sure she will be back looking for it. I want you to tell her I have it and that I want her to call me."

She asked if he wanted to leave the book here for the woman to pick up. And he said he didn't.

"I want the woman to know I have it. And that I'm holding it for her."

He said, "She is short, graying black hair, attractive. Lives in Amherst."

"What's her name?"

"Give me a piece of paper, I'll write it out for you."

She didn't have a piece of paper.

He had a letter in his coat pocket, tore open the envelope and used part of it to write the name Mary on it, the message that he had found her book and wanted to get it back to her, put down his name and address and phone number. Before giving it to the woman, he told her again how important it was.

He could see that she was not impressed. This was not part of her job. She was getting paid to dust and mop, not run a message center.

Olney brushed some strands of hair across his bald spot.

"I want you to tape it up next to the cash register so that whoever comes to work later will see it."

She didn't have any tape.

Olney pulled a five dollar bill from his wallet and laid it on the bar.

"There must be some tape somewhere."

She searched through some drawers and finally found some Scotch tape. And taped the message on the wall by the cash register.

And looked at him.

He gave her the five dollars.

"Her name is Mary. When she comes looking for the book, tell her it is very important that she call me right away."

She folded the bill and tucked it into a side pocket.

"All right. I'll tell her."

"Leave the message taped to the wall until she comes looking for the book."

She said she would.

She wouldn't, of course. He knew that.

In the parking lot, Olney sat in his car for a few minutes debating whether or not to stay there waiting for her to come back looking for her book.

It would be fun to see the expression on her face when she pulled into the parking lot and Olney walked over to say hello.

But it might be days before she remembered. If she remembered at all.

He started the engine and headed for home.

Seventeen

Mary Ostrowski turned the key in the ignition, took a moment for the engine to warm up, fastened her seat belt. And turned on the radio.

That was a mistake. She should not have done that.

She saw Olney look her way, then saw him pull out of his parking place and head for the road. She prepared to follow.

The radio, as always, was tuned to WFCR, the good music station. And she heard the opening bars of *Symphonie Fantastique*. By Berlioz. Of all his works, this was her favorite. And she paused for a moment to tune in the station even better.

She started moving again, went through the parking lot and up to the road, had to wait a few minutes until some cars passed and the road was clear. Then turned right, as Olney had said to do.

She wondered which orchestra this was and who was conducting.

Four years ago, she and Paul had heard it at Tanglewood with the Boston Symphony, Seiji Ozawa conducting. And afterwards they had gone to a party at the Richardsons'. Elody had played the piano. So had Paul. There had been drinks on the terrace. Moonlight. The smell of flowers. Talk of Paris, Italy, London.

That had been a night to remember. It all came back so vividly. She could almost see the faces, hear the laughter,

even remembered what she wore and how nice she had
looked and how young she had felt. Of one man who had
even flirted with her a little and she had pretended not to
notice.

The traffic was heavy. She tried to get her mind back on
her driving. Cars kept passing at what seemed to her to be
an excessive speed.

Most of the people there she had not seen since Paul's
funeral nearly two years ago. And she had not been to a
really good after-concert party since that one at the Rich-
ardson's. And wondered why. Probably her own fault. She
had not been happy for a long time, and people tend to
stay away from unhappy people.

Tanglewood hadn't been as much fun as it had once
been. To enjoy good music you have to be in the company
of someone you're happy to be with.

She remembered saying something like that to Olney.
And he had said it was the same way with fishing.

And she suddenly remembered that she was supposed
to be looking for Highland Road.

She turned around at the next intersection and headed
back.

And felt the first signs of panic.

After two or three miles she came to Highland Road,
and turned on to it. She took the first right, then the next
left. Two miles on that road and she came to a fork. Two
rather narrow dirt roads led left and right, neither of
which looked as if they could possibly lead to a place called
Smiley's.

She went back to the road she had turned off of, took a
right, then a left. A little farther along she entered beautiful farm country. Big green meadows with large patches of
bright yellow flowers. Cows. Barns. Puffy white clouds
floating across a clear blue sky.

She felt like crying. And did, a little.

She passed a farmhouse and saw a woman leaving the house and heading for the garden. Mary stopped the car, backed up, got out, waved.

The woman started toward her and they met halfway.

"Could you tell me how to find a place called Smiley's?"

"What kind of place is it?"

"It's a country store or something. And they serve breakfast."

The woman was about forty-five to fifty years old. Big sunny face, summer dress and apron, and very sorry that she had never heard of a place called Smiley's. You could tell that she would love to be helpful if she only could.

The woman shook her head.

Mary said, "It's in this area somewhere."

The woman shook her head again. She said she had lived in this house for twenty-one years, but she had never heard of a place called Smiley's.

But she had a suggestion.

"Why don't you come on in and we'll see if we can find it in the phone book."

Good idea. They tried it. They went inside, got the woman's phone book, went through it carefully, found no listing for Smiley's.

Mary called telephone information.

Nothing.

The operator said, "We got Sanderston Inn, Saunter's Farm Supplies, and Stanopoli Pizza Parlor. But we do not have a listing for Smiley's."

"It is somewhere in the area of Sanderston Inn. Somewhere between that and the road to Route Twenty."

It could be somewhere on the road to ruin, for all the operator cared.

She said it once more. "We have no listing for Smiley's." And hung up.

There was only one thing left to try, so Mary tried that. She got directions from the woman for finding her way back to Sanderston Inn.

She parked her car in the lot, went around to the side entrance and into the kitchen, found the young man who earlier had told Olney how to get to Smiley's. Asked if he would come outside for a minute.

He came out.

"You remember a little while ago a man asked you about a place nearby that served breakfast?"

He remembered.

"A place called Smiley's?"

"Smiley's?"

"Yes. You called to someone inside and asked him the name of the place and he said it's Smiley's."

"He didn't say it's Smiley's. He said it's Reilley's."

"Reilley's?"

"That's right."

She nodded.

All right. She could see how it happened.

It's Reilley's. 'Sreilley's. Smiley's.

Olney had told her more than once he didn't hear as well as he used to.

And if a man were to hear something a little wrong, he could do worse than come up with something like Smiley's.

Only a man of happy disposition and good cheer would get Smiley's out of 'Sreilley's. She didn't know whether to laugh or cry.

"Would you tell me how to get there, please."

He told her. And she thanked him.

She found Reilley's easily enough. And it was just as Olney had described it.

Gas pumps outside, groceries and a lunch counter inside. Eight or ten tables out back. But she didn't see his car in the parking lot.

The man behind the lunch counter was nice enough, but he didn't remember seeing a large man with dark hair brushed across a bald spot.

"You might check with the waitress out back. He may have eaten out there."

She tried that.

The waitress said she did remember a man like the one Mary described. He had had breakfast there earlier.

"I remember he said he had just remembered something, and left before he had even finished his meal."

"He didn't, of course, say what it was he had remembered or where he was going?"

He hadn't.

Mary said, "Thanks, anyway." And headed for home.

As for the book, Mary didn't remember it until after she had parked her car in front of the house and was ready to get out. She looked down at the seat on the passenger side, where the book should have been. And sat there for a long moment feeling sorry for herself.

Florence was sitting in the side yard. Waiting. Like a concerned parent. But withholding judgment until after first hearing the explanation.

She said, "You didn't come home last night."

That was true.

"I know."

"And there are messages for you on the dining room table."

Mary was too tired and discouraged to protest.

"One is from Mrs. Rhinehart wanting to know why you missed Larry's ten o'clock piano lesson."

"I'll call her."

"And your daughter Rosemary wants you to call her right away."

"All right."

The cats were waiting for her just outside the door.

She said, "C'mon in kids."

They did.

"Don't ask me where I've been."

She got a can of cat food for them and opened it.

"I'll tell you about it later."

She said, "If I tried to tell you about it now I'd probably end up crying."

She called Rosemary. Rosemary said that neither of Cheryl's friends were home and could she bring Cheryl up to spend the day with Mary. And Mary said yes, of course.

Later, when she went outside with a cup of tea and the newspaper, Florence had a few more things to say.

"Well, I hope you at least enjoyed yourself."

"I did, thanks. I enjoyed myself very much."

"You haven't yet explained why you didn't come home. And where you spent the night."

"I know."

She settled into her chair, took a sip of her tea, opened the paper.

"When your daughter called this morning, I didn't tell her you had stayed out all night."

Mary said, "That's too bad. She probably would have been happy to hear it."

She spent most of the afternoon posing for Cheryl and trying to explain why she couldn't adopt her friend, Heather.

"I'm sure that elderly widows living alone are not considered suitable adoption parents."

"She's going to have to be adopted by someone. She told me that. Her social worker told her so."

"Maybe her social worker is wrong."

"She doesn't want to be adopted by someone she doesn't know. If they try to do that to her, she'll just run away."

Mary leaned back and relaxed in her reclining chair. The sun cap partly shielding her face. In the warm sunshine she got so comfortable that she almost dozed off.

Cheryl said, "Maybe some day you will get married again. Then you could adopt Heather."

Mary said, "Anything's possible."

Mary went back to the Sanderston Inn the next morning to look for her book.

She went first to the picnic table where she and Olney had had their morning coffee, but it wasn't there. That was disappointing, but it still left the possibility that someone had turned it in to the lost and found department inside. If there was one.

The front door of the inn was locked, and the sign said that it would open at one o'clock. But she saw two young men inside, so she rapped on the glass and signalled for them to open the door. Which one of them did, reluctantly.

He said, "We're closed, Lady. Open at one o'clock," And was about to shut the door, but she put a foot against it.

So he opened it a bit wider and she went in.

There were two of them, both about nineteen or twenty years old. They had been sweeping or mopping or something, but whatever they had been doing, it could not have been too painful because they had on their faces the look of kids who only a moment ago had been barely able to stop laughing at what was no doubt the funniest thing they had heard for a long time.

She said, "I left a book here yesterday. I would like to know if anyone found a book and turned it in."

One of them turned to his friend, "Did you find a book and turn it in, Charlie?"

Charlie hadn't. Even the possibility seemed hilarious. He said, "I haven't found a book in years."

"Is the manager in?"

They said he wasn't in at the moment. But the question brought a momentary improvement in behavior and it did seem as if they would be able to avoid losing themselves in uncontrollable hysterics at whatever was so amusing.

"Do you have a lost and found department? Or any place where someone would turn in a book they found?"

"Yes. But there are no books in it."

"What time does the manager come in?"

"One o'clock."

"Do you want to look through the lost and found department, or should I wait until the manager gets in?"

The young man shrugged his shoulders, turned, said to his friend, Charlie, "Let's show the lady what's in the bin."

She followed them past the registration desk and around and into the small office. In a corner was a large wooden bin, no cover, and Charlie bent over and looked in.

The other one joined him and they looked in together. And laughed. And Mary had the feeling that she was now in on the continuation of the joke that had been in progress before she arrived.

"Lady," Charlie said, "we got a lot of things in here. But no books."

He started laughing.

He said, "We got a beach ball, two Frisbees, a kid's tennis shoes, socks, towels. Things like that."

He said, "Also," and he reached down into the bin, bringing up the item that had got the kids into hysterics earlier, "A pair of lady's panties found outside just this morning."

He held them up, stretching them at the top. "But I don't think they're your size. They are rather large."

Which they were.

She asked, politely, "Are you sure there is not a small book in there somewhere?"

Charlie bent over and looked once more into the bin. He said, "No, Ma'am. We got a shaving kit, a teddy bear, and a softball."

He held the softball up for her to see.

She said, "Thank you." And left.

She called the Inn from her house later that afternoon and spoke to the manager. He said, rather abruptly, that no one had turned in a book.

She gave him her name and phone number in case anyone did, but she had the feeling he likely was not even bothering to write it down.

There was another message for her on the table when she got back. It was from Mrs. Rhinehart again, who left word that because her son had been so happy Mary had not shown up for yesterday's piano lesson, she had decided to let him quit.

All right.

In the early evening Mary sat in the yard for a while, sipping a glass of wine and planning her next move.

One thing was certain. She would have to go back to Northampton, where Olney lived, apparently, and spend time there looking for him. Soon. Like tomorrow.

She would spend some hours just walking up and down Main Street. Sit for a while in the park. Have coffee or ice cream at one of those little tables on the first floor of Thorne's Marketplace. People said that if you sit there long enough you will sooner or later see everyone in town you know. And another thing to do would be to sit on the terrace of the Hotel Northampton. He would be certain to pass by there sooner or later.

She pictured in her mind how it would be.

She would casually wave. Lean over the railing and ask if he felt like joining her for a drink. He would stop and stare at her as if he could hardly believe it was she. He would push some hair across his bald spot. Then, rather than go inside and come out onto the terrace, he would come climbing over the railing to confront her.

He would say in a loud voice, "Why didn't you follow me?"

She would say, in a softer voice, "Smiley's, for God's sake! How did you come up with a name like Smiley's?"

Then he would grab her a little too hard, hold her a little too tight. The way he had at the inn just after they had got into their room.

If it didn't happen exactly that way, it would happen something like that. There would be a happy ending. She was sure of that. One thing Dr. Whorter said was that you should always believe in happy endings and that you should stay away from people who don't.

87% of those people who believe in happy endings end up with happy endings. As compared to only 19% of those who don't.

After a while she went inside, read some more of the novel, and watched an old movie. One she had already seen several times. *Casablanca.* With Humphrey Bogart, Ingrid Bergman, Claude Rains.

As usual, she cried a little at the end.

Eighteen

How do I love thee? Let me count the ways.
I love thee to the depth and breadth and height
My soul can reach, when feeling out of sight
For the ends of Being and Ideal Grace.
I love thee to the level of every day's
Most quiet need, by sun and candlelight.
I love thee freely, as men strive for Right;
I love thee purely, as they turn from Praise;
I love thee with the passion put to use
In my old griefs, and with my childhood's faith;
I love thee with a love I seemed to lose
With my lost saints, — I love thee with the breath,
Smiles, tears, of all my life! — and, if God choose,
I shall but love thee better after death.

All right.

Olney closed the book, looked out toward the green hills and blue skies and accepted the fact that it was going to take a long time for him to forget that nice woman with the chin tilted up just a bit in a way that reminded him of the beautiful great blue heron.

She should at least have been willing to have breakfast with him. She should at least have done that. She could at least have said she had enjoyed it, admitted that for her it had been only a harmless lark, but fun. And he could have admitted that he had taken it more seriously than he should have, and had even thought it might be the beginning of something permanent.

Anyway, she was a great lover. He would testify to that. Any man who couldn't be happy in bed with a woman like her couldn't be happy in bed with any woman ever.

He looked at the book in his hands and wished there were some way he could get it back to her.

The book was almost new, but had been bought second hand.

On the flyleaf was a message in a woman's handwriting:

> *To Nick. With love.*
> *May you always remember.*
> *Christina*

Nick, whoever he was, apparently had chosen not to remember.

Olney felt bad about that.

How could a man turn away from a woman who loved him and had given him a beautiful book of poems? It was not easy to believe that someone could do that.

He hoped that by now Christina had found herself a good man. A man who could appreciate a woman who liked poetry and was in love. Someone she chose to marry and have children with and who would always remember.

It was another hot afternoon. Almost too hot to sit on the deck. Certainly too hot to go to the lake and expect to catch any fish.

The girls had just finished a Coke and Olney a beer.

Olney said, "I got an idea."

The girls looked at one another. Whatever that idea was, you could be sure of one thing. It would be a dumb idea.

Heather asked, cautiously, "What is it?"

Olney said, "Two things I been intending to do that I should have done long ago."

They looked at one another again. Waited.

"I want to go into town and get a library card. That's something I should have done a long time ago."

He said, "The other thing is that it's time I went to see the Norman Rockwell Museum."

You would not have to be the most astute observer in the world to note immediately that these were not the two most exciting suggestions the girls had ever heard of. And it took them a little while to reach a decision.

However, because there was no one else to sketch, Cheryl said she guessed she'd go with him. If she could take her sketch pad. And if she was going to go, then Heather would go, too. If she could take her basketball and practice dribbling on the sidewalk on the way there and back.

Those were reasonable demands, and Olney agreed to them.

"It's time you kids got some culture."

"Oh, Olney."

Stockbridge is a beautiful little village. Clean, quiet, filled with friendly people. Lots of young mothers and baby carriages. Dogs. Nice old ladies chatting with other nice old ladies in front of the post office or grocery store. Everyone who has lived in town very long knows most of the other people who have lived in town very long. And even if there is someone you don't know, you nod to them anyway.

Lots of money in Stockbridge. Not many poor people. Summer residents swell the population and help keep alive the feeling that New York and Boston aren't too far away.

During the summer the massive influx of tourists is a major problem that most people somehow manage to live with. Not all. Some have to get away for a couple of weeks every summer the way others have to get down to Florida for a week or two every February. Some simply belong to a small support group and when a person is about to crack under the stress, he calls a friend who comes right over to assure him that the tourist season won't last forever.

Things get back to normal after Labor Day.

Olney got his library card, then brushed some hair across his bald spot and told the nice woman behind the desk that he had recently finished reading a book of poetry by someone named Elizabeth Barrett Browning. It was called *Sonnets From The Portuguese*. He asked if she knew of any other books of poetry of that kind.

He said he had never read much poetry.

She asked if he had read Edna St. Vincent Millay, and he said he hadn't.

She got him a small book of poetry called *Second April*. "I think you will like these."

"Thank you."

Heather took out two books on basketball and charged them to Olney's new library card. Cheryl took out a book of Doonesbury cartoons.

At the museum they joined a small group of visitors ready to start their tour. One nice woman, rather stocky and official looking, asked Heather if maybe it wouldn't be better if she left the basketball at the desk while she looked at the pictures. But Heather said she thought maybe she'd just carry it with her. And held it in such a way that anyone could tell she had no intention of bouncing it.

After a moment, the woman said she guessed it would be all right.

The woman who guided the group through the building and talked to them of the paintings and Norman Rockwell was intelligent looking, probably late forties, attractive, and a great admirer of Rockwell. There were only about forty of his paintings on display, she said, even though the museum owned about four or five hundred of his works. You could tell she wished they had room to show all of them.

There were about a dozen people in their group. An older couple in their late sixties, two younger couples, a few women by themselves, looking as if they might be school teachers on vacation, and a pair of newlyweds. He was heavy, bearded, wore blue jeans and had the look of a workingman. She was also wearing jeans, brunette, average height but a bit broader in back than the average woman her height. As they moved along, every once in a while the man gave her a nice little pat on the rear and she gave him an affectionate little hug in return. About four times to each room. A nice touch. Rockwell would have painted them immediately.

Rockwell's medium was oil. The woman said that. And told about the study, preparation, research that went into every work. Photographs, sketches, then the final painting. She pointed out small details that showed how much care the artist had taken. She showed how the paintings demonstrated his sense of humor, sentimentality, his affection for the simple people, the common people, and how he enjoyed exposing the pretentiousness, unwarranted pride, and presumed superiority of those people who thought they were better than other people.

One of her favorite paintings was the one titled *Freedom of Speech*. The story of a Vermont town meeting with one of the ordinary folk, in workingman's clothes, exercising his right to stand up and express his opinion the same as everyone else. Same as the men in white shirts and ties next to him.

A good painting and a good philosophy by anyone's standards.

Another favorite was the one called *Checkers*, one of Rockwell's early paintings, showing a clown playing checkers with a man who looks as if he might be the owner of the circus. And the clown has won. Five checkers still on the board, with three of them, in positions of advantage, belonging to the clown. A woman performer and the ringmaster look on. Another performer is in the background. A dog is asleep at the clown's feet. The clown sits on a box with the figure 5 on it. Five on the box, five checkers, five people.

The painting Cheryl liked best was Norman Rockwell's self-portrait. (The lady said that Rockwell had painted himself a little better looking than he really was, which she thought was forgivable, and laughed. Everyone else laughed, too. They would have done the same, of course.)

Cheryl studied that particular painting for a long time, staying with it even after the rest of the group had moved on to other paintings. Even after the tour guide had led the group into the next room, Cheryl was still standing in front of Rockwell's self-portrait, looking up at it.

It was a scene Rockwell would have loved to paint.

The light was just right. Sunshine came in from the window on her left. What you saw was a little girl in profile, standing transfixed, bent slightly from the waist to get a better view, sketch pad in hand, lost in thought or dream, looking up in awe at the man who had painted all these paintings.

Olney let her stand there for a minute or more, then called to her softly. They caught up with their group and finished the tour.

Before going back to the house, the three of them strolled around town for a while, looking at people. It was a beautiful day, so they were not the only ones strolling around town looking at people. Most of the people seemed to be enjoying themselves. If they glanced his way, Olney always said, "Hi!"

Every time he would look at someone and say "Hi!" the kids would look at one another and shake their heads.

Cheryl said, "Olney, why do you say hello to people you don't even know?"

He said, "It's all right. They don't know me either."

He said, "If you feel like walking down the street and saying hello to people, then go ahead and do it. If they don't like it, that's their problem. Not yours."

He said, "Don't let people decide for you how to feel walking down the street."

He said, "You let people start telling you how to feel walking down the street and pretty soon you'll be letting them tell you how to live your life."

A young woman with long blond hair and being tugged along by a large black dog on a leash looked their way and smiled, and Olney said, "Hi!"

She said, "Hi!"

In the window of one of the small shops they saw some figurines of Rockwell characters and some plates with Rockwell pictures on them. Cheryl wanted to go inside and look at them, so they did. Olney told the shop owner, a man about his age, that they weren't planning on buying anything, just wanted to look at the Rockwell things.

The man didn't mind. He even took time to talk to them.

He had some interesting things to say about the objects he referred to as Rockwell collectibles. He said that the early collectibles had increased a lot in value over the years. Back in about 1971, for instance, a set of four porcelain plates showing Rockwell's *Four Seasons* paintings sold for sixty dollars the set.

He said that now you could sell them for at least ten times that amount.

One interesting thing about that big increase in value, he said, was that the people who bought them years ago did so because they liked them, and not because they suspected someday they would be worth a lot of money. The people who bought the early prints and plates and figurines were not the kind of people who ordinarily bought prints and paintings. They bought Rockwell's work because they liked what he was saying about the good things in life. Simple pleasures. Childhood. Family. Fun. Important occasions like high school graduations and birthday parties.

Olney said he had good feelings about Rockwell because he remembered back when he was nine or ten years old he had had a *Saturday Evening Post* route.

That got the owner a bit excited. He said that he had had one, too, when he was a kid.

"I remember that big white canvas bag with the wide strap that went around your shoulders. It had a wide strap so it wouldn't cut into a kid's shoulders. Remember?"

Olney did.

"I remember the magazine cost five cents."

The man remembered that. "I used to have about forty customers on my route."

"With forty customers," Olney said, "you could make a lot of money." And they laughed together.

"*Boy's Life*," Olney said. "You remember that?"

Of course.

"That was a long time ago."

Olney asked the man how business was and the man said it was good. Especially during the summer.

Before they left, the man said he hoped they'd stop in again.

Olney told him where he lived. "Stop by some time and have a drink on the patio with us."

The man said he would. And did. One Sunday afternoon when he and his wife were out for a walk. The kids were there that day and everyone had a good time.

Olney had another idea. One that the kids liked.
"Maybe we ought to get some ice cream cones to eat on the way back to the house."
"All right."
"But don't get ice cream on the library books."
They said they wouldn't.

On the patio that evening Olney read the book of poems he had got from the library. He liked it. It was easier to read, but still there were lines he found difficult to understand. He wished there were someone he could talk with about the parts he wasn't sure of.
He took Solomon for one last walk in the park, then went inside to see whose turn it was to beat the Red Sox.

Nineteen

Mary Ostrowski went another night to watch one of Pauline's baseball games. This time Pauline's team lost, but in many ways Mary found the game more fun to watch. This time she felt more a part of it, even though she sat in the stands and did little more than look and listen. A few times she did call out a few words of encouragement, taking her cue from whatever those around her were calling out.

This time she gave more attention to the abilities and qualities of the individual players, making note of which women were more likely to hit the ball when it came their turn at bat, and which were more likely to catch the ball if it were hit or thrown in their direction. Which players tried harder, which were more competitive. Things like that.

Trying to become more interested in baseball was in line with another of Dr. Whorter's theories. Mary was trying to achieve what Dr. Whorter referred to as Horizontal Growth.

Horizontal Growth, as different from Vertical Growth.

His theory, as best Mary could understand it, was this:

Vertical Growth is the result of the effort we make to achieve some specific and usually narrow goal that is most important to us at some particular point in life. It is the result of the activity we specialize in in order to gain recognition, self-esteem, financial success, our desired place in society. The means by which we try to be as good as or better than others trying for the same or similar things. Our specialization. There is only one direction: Up.

Football player, weight lifter, concert pianist, inventor, manufacturer, writer, baker, thief. Wife, husband, dancer, sexologist, stockbroker, artist, minister, payroll clerk. And so forth.

In an age when specialization pays off, we specialize. We would be foolish not to.

But in many people's lives there comes that time when the narrow pursuit of vertical goals must be set aside and more attention paid to what is going on around you. Maybe the person you have shared so many years with now feels your life is too narrow. Or no longer cares. Or has left you for someone else. Or has died. Or something.

Maybe the kids have grown up and gone and your life has changed accordingly. The company you worked for for so many years has gone broke and you find the skills you have are out of date. Aged parents, whom you had devoted your life to caring for, have died and left an emptiness. Maybe your social life, that had been so good for so many years, with many lovers and happy times, has suddenly gone flat. Your phone doesn't ring nearly as often as it used to, and now the people you call to invite to dinner almost always have previous engagements.

Or whatever.

The time has now come to reach out horizontally and explore new interests, see new kinds of people, do different kinds of things. Involve yourself in activities that heretofore had held no interest to you. Include more people in your realm of acceptance, and make yourself acceptable to more people. Make your world wider.

The way Dr. Whorter related this theory to people trying not to grow old alone was simply this: It bettered your chances.

You now have more people to choose from. People of a kind you've never known before. Such unusual types as birdwatchers, baseball fans, bridge players, skiiers, beachcombers, and outdoor-camping addicts.

Dr. Whorter made a point of stressing that anything he said about people increasing the number of people they are compatible with and compatible to, applies not only to men looking for women and women looking for men, but for men looking for men and women looking for women. Or even people simply looking for some enjoyable companion to go to a movie with.

In the process of expanding horizontally, you become a bit less judgmental. And, at the same time, a bit more tolerant of those who are. You become a bit less rigid yourself, but a bit more tolerant of those who are.

None of us is perfect.

One of the easiest ways to achieve some Horizontal Growth, according to Dr. Whorter, was to read things a bit different from what you usually read. A newspaper or magazine that is politically a little to the left or right of what you've become accustomed to. Or on some subject that you ordinarily avoid.

Mary tried that. She bought a copy of *Sports Illustrated* and took it home and skimmed through it. She didn't get much from it except the feeling that the people in the stories or interviews seemed rather normal, and in some cases even nice enough. One story about a basketball coach in some college out in the midwest somewhere made him seem somewhat interesting. Probably, once he got home from work, he could be fun to have around the house.

Another thing Dr. Whorter recommended was that you improve your listening habits. He said that most of us are poor listeners. We listen to someone only up to that point where we decide whether or not we like them or agree with them. Then we stop.

But if you want to learn to understand what people are really like, you keep listening until you not only know what they are saying, but why they are saying it. What it is in their personality or background that leads them to have the opinions they have. He said that if you keep that in mind, almost any conversation becomes interesting.

Another thing about listening, according to him, was that you should practice listening to yourself. Listen to what you are saying and why you are saying it. You can sometimes learn a lot from that.

He had some interesting things to say about faces.

Anyone looking for that certain person who they might find enjoyably compatible might start by looking at people's faces. Everyone's face is to some extent an open record of where they've been and what they've done. The person behind the face is responsible for what their face reveals.

No one, of course, is responsible for the shape of his or her nose or mouth or whether or not both eyes focus on the same spot at the same time. Or the chin, eyes, size of the ears. Only for what the person has done to make the face show what it shows.

Over the years, anger or meanness leaves its mark. So do kindness and gentleness. As does worry, unhappiness, fear, tension, joy, hate, cruelty, or passivity. Both frowns and laughter leave their own kinds of marks. As do thought and contemplation. And on some people's faces you can see that the owner doesn't care one way or the other what anyone might think they see there.

Faces, he said, make for interesting reading.

Be sure, he said, to note how often you are right. And how often you are wrong. Sometimes you can learn something about your own prejudices by seeing how you misinterpreted what you felt so sure that someone's face indicated.

Dr. Whorter told of a friend who was married to a woman with an interesting face.

That nice woman had an unfortunate dental condition in which the upper teeth protruded quite a bit more than the lower ones. The face was fairly thin and had high cheekbones. Nothing there that kept her from looking attractive, which she certainly was, but which did limit the kinds of expression she could show on her face.

She could scowl, frown, show anger or annoyance. Provided she did not open her mouth. But should she try to say something, it was not possible, because of the dental structure, for her mouth to do anything except open up into a big grin. A happy smile.

To open her mouth was to laugh.

Her husband said she was a joy to live with. And mentioned times like the day he got home from a hard day's work and she tried to tell him she was sorry about denting the fender of their new car on the side of the freshly painted garage door and within seconds the two of them were laughing and hugging and dancing around the room.

Once she went to the department store to complain because the vacuum cleaner she had bought didn't work, and she and the salesman ended up with their arms around one another and tears of laughter rolling down their faces.

Her husband said that one night he got home from work and she had to break the news that the bank had called again about the overdue mortgage payment and that the plumber had refused to come fix the sump pump in the basement until he got paid for fixing it the last time, and before she had finished telling him those things, he was laughing so hard he couldn't stop and they opened up a bottle of champagne and invited the Friedmans, their next door neighbors, over for a party.

He said she was a problem, though, during income tax time. He made her go visit her mother the day he went to work on his taxes. He was afraid that she might come in to say something or other and he'd get laughing, end up telling the truth, and invite the tax auditors to stop by for a party the next time they happened to be in the area.

No self-respecting orthodontist would ever alter the tooth alignment of anyone with a dental structure of the kind that makes it impossible for a woman to open her mouth without looking happy and loving.

That was Dr. Whorter's opinion.

Twenty

The morning got off to a bad start, then got worse as the day went on.

The kids came up the driveway with Solomon limping along beside them, bleeding from a cut paw. Heather said that he was on his way down to meet them and had walked through some glass from a broken bottle by the side of the road. They felt worse than Solomon did, probably.

Olney said, "It wasn't your fault. Don't feel bad about it."

He washed out the cut, put some medicine on it, and used a clean handkerchief for a bandage.

"In a day or two he'll be as good as new."

"We picked up the glass," Heather said, "so he won't step on it again."

"Good."

The kids gave him a lot of sympathy and attention, which Solomon didn't seem to mind. Then after a while Heather went over to practice her free-throw shots and Olney and Cheryl went to work on their cartoons.

Cheryl wanted to try a new sketch. She wanted to show him reading a newspaper with just his head showing. That would not be easy, but she could do it.

All right. That fit with the idea Olney had, anyway. He had been reading the astrology column in the *Berkshire Eagle* and had been impressed with how seriously the readers took it.

This was the cartoon.

"According to this letter, she'd lived with him for six months."
"She left because she found that he had lied to her."
(Sue) "In what way?"
"He said he was a Capricorn."
"But it turned out he was a Taurus."

Cheryl said she thought Olney's cartoon ideas were getting too serious.
"You should be getting funnier."
He thought so, too.
"But I've had a lot on my mind lately. None of it funny."
Olney had another idea that he had got from reading the newspaper. This one from the woman columnist who gave advice to people with marital problems. One wife had written in to say that she and her husband kept their romantic feelings alive by going every once in a while to a motel for the night, as they used to do before they were married.
The idea needed a little work, but it would be something like this.

"She said they used to spend one night a week in a motel."
"It saved their marriage, but was getting too expensive."
(Sue) "So what did they do?"
"They simply moved the TV into the bedroom."
"And put white paper bags over the drinking glasses."

He suddenly hit a hand hard against the side of his head.
"What's the matter, Olney?"
He shook his head. "I just remembered something."

It was something that even a retired plumber should have had sense enough to think of before this.

"I've got to go out for a while."

"Where are you going?"

Olney said, "I'm going to a place called Sanderston Inn. I just want to look at something."

What he realized, after this long time, was that it would be easy to find out the name of that nice woman whose book of poetry he had. Anyone with any brains would have thought of it long before this.

"There's more Cokes upstairs. And sliced ham and cheese in the refrigerator. Cookies in the bread box."

He said, "Make sure Solomon has water to drink. And try to keep him off the foot for a while."

She said they'd do that.

"I'll be back in a couple hours."

"We'll be here."

"Make some sketches of Solomon with the bandage on his paw."

"All right."

The woman behind the registration desk at Sanderston Inn was about fifty years old. She had a thin face, glasses, a tight smile, and a look of disapproval. The man in the office behind her, presumably her husband, was a little older, medium height, balding, with a short bristly mustache.

Olney assumed that they were co-managers of the inn.

He gave them a nice hello and a big smile.

The woman asked, "Can we help you?"

The registration book was not on the counter, as he had expected it would be. Olney saw it on the table in the office behind her.

All Olney wanted was to take a look at just one page of it.

Before he could say anything. The woman said, "We have no vacancies until after Labor Day." And he suddenly realized that he was maybe in trouble.

He brushed some strands of hair across the bald spot.

He told them the truth.

He said, "I'm in a bit of trouble."

She offered no sign of concern, but did raise her eyebrows ever so slightly.

"I need to ask a favor of you." And moved more hair across the bald spot.

The husband moved part way out of the office, head cocked to one side, listening. Standing ready to support his wife in her opinion that whatever favor the man was about to ask was one which they could not possibly grant. For a number of reasons.

"What kind of favor do you want?"

You could tell that the kind of person who asked favors did not rank very high on her list of high-quality people.

Olney reminded himself to relax and not jump to any hasty conclusions.

These were probably two nice people. And because they were involved in something as complex and difficult as managing an inn, they couldn't be expected to jump at the opportunity to help everyone who happened to come in asking for a favor.

Had the registration book been out on the counter, Olney could simply have opened it to the date of July 19 and read the name of the woman he was looking for.

"I'd like to look at the registration book."

The husband now moved out to the counter. He looked at his wife, shook his head, said to Olney, "We can't let you do that."

For a few moments Olney looked at them and they looked back at him.

Olney said, "I can understand why you ordinarily wouldn't let people look at it, but this happens to be very important to me."

He said, "I need to get the last name of the nice woman I spent the night with on the nineteenth of July."

They just looked at him. There was no change of expression.

"She got the room for herself, originally," Olney said. "She signed the registration book. All I want is to see her last name."

The woman frowned and scowled disapprovingly. Her husband shook his head. Shook his head several times.

"We can't help you."

Olney tried to stay relaxed. He reminded himself once more that these were no doubt nice people. Under other circumstances he would have been happy to buy them a drink or two and tell them about the time he had installed the new boiler downstairs and run pipes out to where they were adding the extra space to the dining area. And of the unusual problems they had encountered. Even though they weren't managing the inn back in those days, they likely would have found his story interesting.

Olney said, "All right. I guess I don't need to see the registration book. Just look on the page for July nineteen and read me her last name."

They looked at one another, smiled, shook their heads simultaneously to show that they were firmly in agreement.

You could tell that the answer was no. Never.

"Her first name is Mary. She is from Amherst. We had dinner together on the nineteenth of July. She was able to get a room for us only because of a last minute cancellation."

The look on the woman's face became even more disapproving. She did not like what she was hearing.

"It is against our policy to reveal the names of our guests." And she smirked just slightly.

"Moreover, we would never approve of a woman renting a room for herself, then later taking men up to it."

The husband nodded his head to show that his wife was correct regarding Inn policy in matters such as this.

"I need to see the book," Olney said, "because I lost contact with the woman and need to learn her last name so I can find her."

He said, "She told me her last name, but I didn't hear it."

The man crowded to the front, pushing his wife aside.

He spoke very firmly. He said, "You are not going to see the book. Nor will I give you any information about anything in the book. So you might as well leave right now."

Olney brushed some hair across the bald spot.

"I intend to see it."

The woman now pushed her husband aside. And gave the final answer.

"Go. Go before I call the police."

She pushed her husband ahead of her and they went back to their office.

Olney had no choice. He knew that.

If something has to be done, then you have to do it. There is no other way. He had learned that years ago.

That is the way it is now and will always be.

Police or no police, he was going to see that book.

At age sixty-five, you don't leap across a counter top. What you do, as Olney did, is scramble up on top, then drop down on the other side. He moved quickly into the office, brushed the woman aside, headed for the book.

The husband grabbed the book before Olney got to it.

The woman screamed. She ran to the counter and screamed again. And yelled at someone to call the police.

The man was backed up next to the wall, holding the book behind him.

The woman was still screaming.

"If you don't give me the book," Olney said, "I'll have to take it from you."

The man was not large. He wore glasses. He didn't look very strong. You'd feel bad about hitting a man like this.

Olney turned around and saw them coming. There were two of them. One leaped over the counter, one came through the side door. They were young. One was about thirty years old and big. Bigger than Olney, even. The other was in his middle twenties, slender and quick.

It was the big one who came through the door, and Olney got him straight on, knocking him part way back out the door.

Before he could turn around, the younger one got him hard on the side of the face. Olney went down, hitting his head on the side of a large wooden bin.

It took a moment to clear his head.

As he started to get up, the husband stepped in front of him and tried to push him back down again.

That helped.

Olney got up anyway and pushed the husband into the young man, which got him out of the fight temporarily. And gave Olney time to deal with the big man once more.

He got him hard this time. Twice. Then tried to turn and duck at the same time.

The young one got him hard on the right side of the face once more and again Olney bounced against the cabinet, but this time staying on his feet. He came back, while the kid was off balance, and got in a good punch. And the kid backed away.

Then Olney bent down and picked up the registration book from the floor where the husband had dropped it.

The woman was now back in the picture.

She was yelling, "Let him see the book! Let him see the book!"

Good.

That was all Olney wanted to do. See the goddam book.

He looked around. Felt warm blood run across his lips. Took some deep breaths. Felt his heart pounding.

He looked at the big one and the young one. He said, "Either of you make a move this way and I'll really hurt you."

The woman yelled again. "Let him see the book."

Olney held the book in his hands. Looked at the kids. It would take more than just the two of them to get the book away from him. He wanted to make sure they knew that.

The woman said, "You men stay right where you are. We've already called the police."

All right.

Olney ran a hand across his eyes. Wiped a sleeve across his mouth. Tried to slow down the heavy breathing. Kept his eyes on the kids.

They were crouched, waiting. You could see that they wanted another chance at him.

In a calmer voice, the woman said, "You men stay right where you are. Everything is under control. Let him see the book."

She said to Olney, "They have already called the police."

He took a moment to run a hand across his eyes again. Then opened the book. Turned pages until he got to July nineteen. All the time keeping an eye on the two kids.

On the page he was looking for, he saw the names of three couples, one with lines drawn through them.

The cancellation.

Below that, he found what he was looking for. In the small neat and legible handwriting of the kind you would expect a lady like her to have.

Mr. and Mrs. Olney Heebert.
Northampton, Mass.

All right.

He closed the book, pitched it onto the desk, and looked at the kids.

"If you kids want to finish this, come on out to the parking lot."

The woman said, "You men stay right here."

They did as they were told.

Olney brushed past the big man, walked into the lobby and through it, past about a dozen people. Workers, guests, others who had been drinking at the bar. They made way for him.

One young waitress, as he passed, was kind enough to say, "Your nose is bleeding."

He said, "Thanks." And got out a handkerchief.

He waited a moment or two in the parking lot, but the kids didn't come out.

He got into his car, pulled out onto the road, turned left and headed for home.

He had not gone far before he saw a police car coming from the opposite direction, blue light flashing. In his rear-view mirror he saw it slow down and signal for a right turn into the parking lot of the Sanderston Inn.

Olney turned onto a small country road and found a place where he could pull off to the side. He walked down to a brook, wet his handkerchief in the cold water and pressed it against his nose until the bleeding stopped. Sat on a rock and took a few moments to give some thought to what had happened.

He said, "God damn!" Then followed that with some other expressions of the kind you learn in the army and never really get out of your system.

He had been lucky. He admitted that.

He said, "You're getting too old to fight. You should know that."

He said, "You could have got beat up real bad. Almost did."

Olney got back into the car and looked at himself in the mirror. The nose was all right, but the bruise high on the cheekbone was already swollen and turning color. That would be there for a while.

He realized, on the way home, that he had handled things badly from the beginning. What he should have done was turn the book over to someone at the inn, with a note in it from him saying he was sorry he had ruined everything, and leaving his name and address. Sooner or later she would have remembered where she left the book, would have gone back for it, and called him. Probably.

Maybe.

The kids asked him how he had got the big bruise on his face and he told them the truth.

"I got into a fight."

They didn't say anything at first, just looked at him.

"Did you win?"

He said, "I don't know. I suppose so. There were two of them."

"Why did you get into a fight?"

He said that it was a long story. Would take too long to explain.

Otis, when he got home, asked about the bruise.

Brenda asked about the bruise.

DeeDee asked about the bruise.

He told them all the same thing. That he had got into a fight. He didn't say why or where. It was a long story. But he always remembered to point out that there had been two of them. As big as he was and younger. He was lucky he didn't get hurt.

Later, sitting on the deck with his beer and cigar, he thought about it some more.

Mr. and Mrs. Olney Heebert!

He shook his head. Laughed a little.

Cheryl asked what he was laughing about.

He said he wasn't really laughing. He was mostly just shaking his head.

About the time the Children's Chimes finished the last tune, DeeDee came down to the deck to wait for Charles. She was wearing a formal white evening gown, looking as beautiful as it is possible for a young woman to look. She said she was going with Charles to a benefit dinner-dance at Blantyre, a very high-class resort on the edge of town, a formal affair hosted by the Fitzpatricks.

Charles pulled into the driveway in a long, low, expensive-looking sports car of one kind or another. Olney didn't know what kind. He had long ago stopped caring about the names of sports cars. He wasn't even sure they were still called sports cars.

Charles was about six feet tall, blond, good looking, athletic build. With a look of self-assurance. He was quite satisfied to be what he was. Or something. All topped off by a nice smile.

He shook hands with everyone, apologized for not having time to sit with them for a while. He no doubt noticed Olney's bruise, but was too polite to ask how he had got it.

Everyone said things like, "Have a good time." Or "Enjoy yourselves." Then he and DeeDee headed for the car.

Before he opened the door on her side, Charles reached down into the seat and brought up a corsage. He pinned it on her, kissed her lightly on the lips.

Olney felt that was not right.

He should have given her the corsage here on the patio so everyone could say how beautiful it was and how nice it looked on her dress.

He felt that all of them in some small way had been insulted.

Norman Rockwell could not have painted that scene of the handsome well-bred young man standing beside his very expensive convertible pinning a corsage on the beautiful and poised young woman. Only an illustrator employed by an advertising agency with automotive contracts could have done that. And it would certainly not have been acceptable as a cover for the *Saturday Evening Post*.

In a Rockwell painting the young man would have been shy, awkward, uncertain. The car would have been older, or had a borrowed look to it, and the girl, instead of being poised and beautiful would have been a little too thin, or something, and both proud and scared at the prospect of attending her first big dinner-dance party. The corsage would not have been large or fancy, but she would have loved it.

There was, however, something there that Rockwell would have loved to use for one of his *Post* covers. It was the look on the face of the very tall young man, Adam's apple just a bit too large, hands too big, dark rimmed glasses, thin face, wearing shorts and tennis shoes, standing there, holding a basketball and watching the handsome and formally dressed young man in his expensive sports car drive away with the young princess.

That scene was a short story all by itself.

This had not been a great day for Mary Ostrowski, either.

She had gone to Northampton, as planned, had spent an hour sitting at one of the small tables at Thorne's

Marketplace, then had walked around town for a while. She had sat in the park a long time, keeping an eye on all the passersby, watching the young mothers and their children.

And thinking about her own.

Gregory would never marry. She felt certain of that. He would go on making his music and living with different women for a few indifferent years. Then someday he would feel that his career was enough and that kids would be a problem.

Not likely that she would get any grandchildren from Pauline, either. She probably wouldn't marry again.

Rosemary had already said that one offspring, Cheryl, was enough.

Cheryl would grow up and marry someday and have children, but by then Mary wouldn't be around to see them. Maybe.

She watched two four-year-olds throwing a ball back and forth. And a little girl learning to ride a two-wheel bicycle falling down and then getting back up. And falling down again. And getting back up again.

She left the park, walked down Main Street once more, then had a sandwich and two leisurely glasses of wine at the sidewalk café of the Northampton Hotel. Still no sign of a broad and balding retired plumber. Then she went inside and asked the nice woman behind the bar to give her three dollars worth of dimes.

In the phone booth in the lobby she called all the Heeberts in the phone book, as well as all the Hibberts, Heebers, Hubers, and Huberts. None of them knew of a plumber named Olney. One, a Hibbert, had a brother who was a plumber, but he was married, had red hair, and lived in Connecticut.

There was still time to try one more thing. So she tried that. On her way home she went out of her way to stop at the Sanderston Inn to ask if anyone had turned in a book of poetry that she had left on a picnic table outside.

The woman behind the desk said no. No one had.

"Do you know if anyone has been here inquiring about a woman named Mary? Maybe saying that he had a book that belonged to her?"

The woman, who had already started to turn away, now turned back and looked at her. Then she turned again and called to her husband.

The husband came to the counter and the two of them looked at Mary in silence for several long moments.

The man asked, "Is he broad, dark hair, bald spot?"

"Yes."

The woman asked the next question.

"Were you here recently, rented a room one night, then invited a man up to your room to spend the night with you?"

She could hardly believe it.

"Yes." She said, "Oh my God, yes! I did that."

She said, "Yes. That was me. And that was him."

They just looked at her.

"Was he here? Did you get his name?"

She could tell by the looks on their faces that the answer was no.

"He was here earlier today," the woman said. "He started a fight. We had to call the police."

Oh, dear!

"Started a fight?"

"Yes."

"Was he hurt?"

"Some."

"Was he arrested?"

"No, he got away before the police arrived."

Good. That was good.

"Why did he start a fight?"

"He wanted to see the registration book and we wouldn't let him."

"Didn't you get his name? Or learn anything at all about him?"

They hadn't. Not only that, they didn't want to talk about it anymore.

They both headed back to the office. Then the woman turned and came back to the counter with one final thing to say.

She stood in front of Mary and said it in a stern, even threatening tone of voice.

"Don't you ever, ever try to rent a room here again. If you do, we will call the police. We do not want your kind of person here."

She turned and went into the office.

So that was that.

Mary stood there for a moment, couldn't think of anything more to do or say, so headed back to her car.

She realized, on her way home, that it would have been better if the police had got there in time to arrest him.

She could have gone to bail him out. They could have been reunited at the police station. Maybe even in his jail cell.

That would have been something to remember.

Something to laugh about over the years.

Their being reunited in a jail cell and her bailing him out.

Twenty-one

The bruise on the side of Olney's face stayed sore and swollen for a few days, then gradually disappeared. But the recollection of the way he got it stayed with him. He remembered the fight and what he had seen in the registration book and didn't know whether to laugh or cry.

Mr. and Mrs. Olney Heebert.
Northampton, Mass.

One thing he was sure of was that there was no way he could ever again go back to the inn and inquire about a woman named Mary who might be looking for a book she had left there.

Just thinking about it depressed him. He was tired. Ready to give up. So he did. He gave up.

He mentioned to Solomon one morning that he thought it was time to make some changes in his life.

He found the real estate woman's business card in the desk drawer, studied it for a moment, had a little talk with himself.

He said, don't do anything hasty. Then a moment later said that doing something hasty was exactly what he was in the mood to do.

He dialed her number.

If you want to make a big change in your life, you can't sit around and think about it, or you won't make it.

The woman remembered him, of course.

He said, "I wanted to check once more on the price you said I could get for the house if I ever decided to sell it."

She mentioned a price a bit higher than the one she had given him the first time.

"That's not enough."

She said she could probably talk the buyer into offering a little more than that. And mentioned a figure the buyer might pay if he had to.

Olney said, "Maybe I'll just put the house on the open market and let everyone bid on it."

She said she'd get back in touch with him soon. Maybe tomorrow evening.

"All right."

He made another call. This one to an old friend in Northampton. Pete Henderson, who sold campers. Olney told him he wanted to buy another camper. Pete said he had one in stock just like the one Olney had got rid of a year ago, except that it was a later model. Olney said he'd try to get over there to look at it in a day or two, but Pete had a better idea.

"I'll have my son, Ben, drive it over and let you try it out for a few days and see how you like it."

"That sounds like a lot of trouble for you."

"Not at all. If you're going to be home Sunday, he'll bring it over. His friend can follow in a car and bring Ben back."

Olney said he'd be here. Gave Pete the address and directions. Then asked, "How's the fishing been?"

Pete said it had been real good in the spring and early summer, but hadn't been good lately. Olney should get over soon, though, and they'd try it together.

Olney said he would, and they hung up.

Always a pleasure to fish with Pete. He fished hard and swore hard. God help those fish who either didn't bite or got hooked and then got away. They really caught hell from Pete.

Olney went down to the deck and found Brenda there having her second cup of coffee. She was feeling good this morning, she said, mostly because her novel was coming along so well.

"Thanks to you, actually."

She said, "From the day you rented me the apartment, everything has simply fallen into place. I haven't had to do anything except go upstairs and put it down on paper. And all I'm waiting for now is to see how it ends. And I should learn that Sunday at Tacy Van Rensselaer's big party."

All right.

"You're in it, you know."

"That's all right with me," Olney said, "as long as you call me Wes. Or Hank."

"I was planning to call you Jeff."

He thought about that. Jeff wasn't too bad. But still not right.

"How about Jim?"

She laughed, said she could do that, finished her coffee.

"I had a long talk with Harry, yesterday."

"That's what he told me."

"He likes you."

She said, "That's too bad, really. Because I'm not the kind of woman he's looking for."

"Are you sure/"

"Yes."

She told about having been married once before, that it hadn't worked, that she felt no need to try again.

"Harry is a romantic. What he is looking for is a woman who wants to settle down in a little house on the edge of town with a garden and kids and a dog."

All right. A man could do worse. But no matter.

"One thing I wanted to mention," Olney said, "is that I'm selling the house. I'm going to tell you and DeeDee and Otis, but ask you not to tell the kids. That won't be easy to do. I'll want to pick the right time to tell them myself."

She was sorry to hear he was selling the house.

"I hope you don't regret it."

He said, "I might. Who knows?"

They talked about other things for a while. Then he excused himself and went inside to make a phone call.

He did something that was out of character, but he felt like doing it, so he did it.

He didn't tell Harry there was a woman he should meet, instead he said that he had had lunch with DeeDee's mother some time ago and had enjoyed himself very much. He wanted to do something nice for her.

"She's a great person, kind of temporarily down on her luck. A good mother with good kids, but not much money."

What he asked Harry to do was go personally to the house and find out what kind of air conditioner the house needs. He said he wanted to give it to her as a gift.

Harry liked that. He would even give it at cost. "It's the least I could do for DeeDee's mother."

"You don't need to do that," Olney said.

"I got a lot of money coming in soon, and I want to use some of it to make DeeDee's mother and the kids a bit more comfortable during the hot weather."

He gave Harry the address and suggested he go there in the early afternoon so he could meet the kids, too, and get their ideas about whether or not they wanted air conditioning.

Harry said he'd do that. And they said good-bye and hung up.

So much for that.

He liked Harry, and when you like someone, you don't pass up the chance to do something nice for them.

He and Rhonda would make a good pair.

Before going back to the patio, Olney got a bag of ice and a dozen cans of beer to put in the cooler for guests.

Two guests had already showed up, but neither drank beer, so Olney went back inside and brought out some Cokes.

Heather was already practicing and Cheryl was waiting with her sketch pad. Olney took his place in the chair and she went to work.

Otis came down, said hello, sat down and opened his newspaper. Olney said hello, then said he couldn't talk because he was being sketched.

"I know." Otis said, "Try not to move so much."

DeeDee came onto the deck and took a chair.

Cheryl said, "You're moving again."

"Sorry."

Cheryl said to DeeDee, "Olney can't talk now. He's being sketched."

She could see that. "Good morning, Olney. And you don't need to answer."

"All right."

DeeDee had her radio with her. She turned it on, then down low so it wouldn't bother anyone.

The music was awful. Olney tried not to hear it.

Otis said, "I like your radio. Charles buy it for you?"

She had brought a magazine with her. She turned a page.

"No, I bought it myself." And turned another page.

"He gave me the money for it, of course."

After several long moments of silence, she asked, "Do you still see that woman you used to live with? The one who used to go with you on all those protest marches and things?"

"Every once in a while."

"You spent all that money on her and then when you split up she kept the apartment. That's what I call getting a lousy deal."

He said he didn't mind. And turned back to the paper.

Heather was over to ask if Otis wanted to come play some basketball. But he was busy reading something in the newspaper.

"It says here that the Historical Room of the Stockbridge Library has acquired a letter written by Catherine Sedgwick to a Lydia Maria Francis Child of Boston, an ardent abolitionist."

In the general direction of DeeDee, he said, "You should read things like this. When you become a member of one of the old families in town you will no doubt sooner or later be appointed to the library committee and be involved in important matters of this kind."

Heather said, "Why don't you put your paper away and come yell at me for not keeping my elbow in."

Olney liked that. That was a good line. He moved a little, laughing at it.

Cheryl put away her sketch book

She said, "Olney?"

DeeDee said, "If Otis won't play basketball with you, Heather, I will. If you'd like."

Heather accepted that, of course. And they headed for the court.

Cheryl said, "Olney? Do you want to take a walk?"

"A walk?"

"I don't like arguing."

All right. He felt the same way.

"Sure. Solomon needs some exercise. We can take him over to the park and let him run for a while."

They could do that if he wanted to. But what she had in mind was maybe walking into town and getting an ice cream cone.

He said, "We can do both."

He asked Otis if he wanted to join them for an ice cream cone. Otis said thanks, but it was too early for ice cream.

Solomon came along without even being asked.

Rhonda called that evening to say Harry had come by to see what kind of air conditioning she'd like.

"I thank you. But why are you doing this?"

First, he explained that he was about to make a lot of money by selling the house for much more than he had paid for it. That had made him feel like doing something nice for someone, and she had come to mind.

He said, "Also, I'm trying to help Harry. The end of summer is always a slow time for air-conditioner salesmen. So I want to throw a little business Harry's way."

He said, "I used to be in business myself. I know what it's like."

Then he spent a while talking about what a nice person Harry was. One of the few people he had met in a long while he really enjoyed having around.

She spent a while herself talking about what a nice person Harry was.

"The kids loved him. They liked his jokes and his coin tricks."

She said, "He's invited us all out to dinner tomorrow night."

"That's nice."

She said, "I'm sorry you're selling the house."

Which reminded him of something else. He said he had some furniture he wasn't using and would like to give it to someone.

"I got a big overstuffed chair and a couple straightback chairs, a lamp and two small tables. You can have them if you want them. And if you can't use them, you can give them to someone who needs them."

He said he'd get them over to her sometime soon. As soon as he found someone with a small truck.

After they hung up, he called Harry's number.

Harry said he didn't want to take Olney's money for the air conditioner. He wanted to make Rhonda a gift of it himself. Olney said he insisted on paying for it, but would let Harry sell it at cost.

"You have to let a man do something he feels like doing," Olney said. "And this is something I want to do."

He asked if Harry knew where he could borrow a pickup truck to use to take a few pieces of furniture over to Rhonda.

Harry said his company had one. He could get it any day when it wasn't in use. Like Sunday.

"Sunday?"

"Sure." And Harry asked if Olney were going to Tacy's big party.

"No. Are you?"

"No. So I'll bring the truck around sometime Sunday."

"Good."

So much for that.

Things were beginning to fall into place.

The real estate agent called Saturday evening to say that the party who wanted to buy the house was willing to pay the price Olney wanted.

"All right."

"I'll bring some papers around tomorrow for you to sign."

Olney said he couldn't do it tomorrow.

"I've got to move furniture tomorrow. Better make it Monday."

Monday would be all right. "Any special time?"

"Any time is all right with me. I'll be here all day."

Twenty-two

Otis said he couldn't believe that Olney was really selling the house.

"I can't imagine ever seeing this deck and you not sitting on it. Drinking beer and smoking cigars. And Solomon lying alongside you."

Olney said that that was what was going to happen.

He had finished his second cup of coffee, had lit a cigar and was waiting for the kids to show up. Otis had come done and had stopped to chat for a moment or two before getting on his way to wherever it was he was going.

"You will always be here, Olney."

"Not after the end of October."

"Always."

Otis said, "Years from now people will be talking about the house on Clark Street. The big yellow house on the corner. They will say that whenever there is a full moon, at night you will see a large man sitting in a chair on the deck behind the house, having a can of beer and a small cigar. And talking to a large black dog lying beside him."

Olney liked that. He laughed. Brushed a bit of hair across his bald spot.

"I hope I don't scare anyone."

"You won't," Otis said. "But if you offer them a chair and a can of beer, they'll turn it down."

"Maybe so," Olney said. "But at least I'll have offered them one."

Otis asked if he had broken the news to the girls yet.

"No. And please don't say anything to them until I've had the chance to take them aside and talk to them about it. Maybe get some ice cream cones and go sit in the park. And I'll break the news to them."

All right.

"What do you plan to do?"

Olney said he wasn't sure. "Travel a bit. Get away from the area for a while."

Otis said, "I hope nothing's wrong."

Olney liked that. An expression of concern. He said no, nothing was wrong.

"I just want to do more with my life than sit here on the deck all day."

Otis asked point blank if it had anything to do with the fight Olney had gotten into not long ago. And hadn't wanted to talk about.

That was coming too close. Olney changed the subject. "How come you're so dressed up this morning?"

This was the first time Olney had seen him with a coat and tie.

The reason was that Otis had to meet with his lawyer and the people he was buying the house from and had a number of other errands to do. Plus going to court for the hearing on his petition to learn who his real mother was. He said, "I've got a pretty full day."

Both his adoptive parents had died in an airplane crash last year.

"Do you think you'll find out who your real mother was? Or is?"

Otis didn't know. Seemed almost not to care too much.

"It never really bothered me that I didn't know who my real parents were. So, if I don't find out, that's all right."

That seemed to be a good attitude to take.

"It's been fun," Otis said, "knowing that you had a mother somewhere in the area, but wouldn't know her if you saw her."

Olney tried to imagine how that would be. He found it difficult.

"And a father, too," Otis said. "And maybe brothers and sisters, aunts and uncles."

He said, "My mother, adoptive mother, that is, let me know early that I had been adopted. She told me all she knew, which was that a young woman in the area, pregnant, wanted to place her child for adoption right after it was born. It was a private adoption, not handled by an agency."

He said, "They never met the woman, of course, and never felt they needed to know anything about her."

Olney liked that. He would have wanted it the same way.

"It was something my parents and I joked about while I was growing up. They'd say, don't make fun of that little old lady in shabby clothes and tennis shoes, she might be your mother."

They both laughed a little.

"If I came home complaining about the umpire being so blind he couldn't tell a ball from a strike, they'd remind me to watch my tongue. The old man might be my father."

That was good.

"I never outgrew it," Otis said. "I almost shouted at some woman I nearly ran into last week because she pulled out in front of me without signaling. Then I could practically hear my mother reminding me that the woman might well by my aunt. Aunt Martha, maybe."

Anything's possible.

Olney said, "There was a picture of a kid on the front page of the *Berkshire Eagle* today. Saved some kid from drowning up on Onota Lake. Might be a cousin of yours."

Otis said, "Possibly. Maybe one of Uncle Charlie's boys. They're all good swimmers."

Then Otis said he had to go. Said he wouldn't be back until late afternoon, probably.

Olney said, "I'll be here. And good luck in court."

Otis said, "I'll let you know how it turns out."

The kids still hadn't shown up, so Olney took a little walk around the property.

The neighbors on his left had a high hedge on their property line, so Olney had never got to know them very well. And the people at the back of his lot had a row of small trees along their line that pretty much blocked his view of them. And vice versa.

Too bad that people put up fences and hedges. It would be more fun if you could be sitting outside on a warm afternoon and if you saw your neighbors you could wave and invite them over for a beer of something.

He spent a few minutes in the garden, said some nice things to the plants about how well they were doing, started back toward the deck. Got an idea.

From where he stood, there was a good view of the house and deck. And two things came to mind. One was how much better the house looked than it did when he bought it. And second, that it would be good to have a picture or painting of the house and deck to keep over the years to remind him of some of the good times there.

He had in mind a certain young artist who could draw him the sketch he had in mind. She was, in fact, just that very moment coming up the driveway. Carrying her sketch pad and accompanied by a tall frizzy-haired nice thirteen-year-old black basketball player.

They all said hello and things like that. It was rather early, but they both accepted a can of Coke. Olney said it was too early for a can of beer, but he opened up one anyway, just to be sociable. Then he lit a cigar and they talked a while before Heather headed for the basketball court and Cheryl got ready to work on cartoons.

Olney didn't feel like working on cartoons today. Even retired people, he said, are entitled to have a day off every once in a while.

"Can you draw houses?

She said, "Sure." She had never tried drawing houses but she knew she could.

"Why?"

He led her to the place where the view of the house was just what he wanted. He said, "What I'd like you to do is make me a drawing of the house and the deck and everything and I'll pay you some money for it."

She was looking at the house with the critical eye of an artist. Olney had to remind himself that she was only ten years old.

"We'll have to buy some things, of course. An easel big enough to hold a big pad. And different kinds of pencils. Maybe even brushes and tubes of paint, or whatever."

He said, "It doesn't have to be perfect. And I'm in no hurry for it."

He had in mind a lot of money.

"If it's all right with your mother, we can go into Pittsfield some day next week and buy you a car full of art supplies."

She was sure it would be all right with her mother.

Then she took four or five steps to her left and a bit nearer the house, studied the house from that angle, and announced that she liked this view better.

All right.

He moved one of the tables out to that spot so she could make some tentative sketches, then went back to his chair and what was left of his beer.

So much for that.

Now he had to think of something big to do for Heather.

DeeDee came down.

She didn't have her radio with her, and she didn't plan to lie on her blanket and work on her sun tan. She had come down just to sit for a while.

Solomon got up and came over to be patted.

The cut on his paw had healed days ago, Olney said. "I'd take the bandage off, but he likes it on. People keep asking him if he's all right."

She scratched behind his ears, said, "You're not so dumb, Solomon."

She waved to Heather, asked what Cheryl was doing out there in the yard, heard the explanation, then settled back in her chair. For a while they just sat there relaxing. Feeling good. Feeling the sun on their bare skin. Looking off to where the green hills and blue sky just sat there sort of showing off.

"How was the big party at Blantyre the other night?"

"Most people liked it, I suppose."She stretched her legs out farther. "I didn't care for it."

She said, "Too many people. All of them drinking too much. Everyone acting as if they were big and important. I got bored after a while."

She said, "One interesting thing was that I had gone there about a year ago looking for a waitressing job. The man who interviewed me said he thought I was too young. I lied to him and said I was nineteen, but he still said no."

An old memory came barging in. Olney laughed.

He said, "I know the feeling."

He said, "I remember when I had just got out of high school and was looking for a job. Someone said the local plumber was looking for a helper, so I went to see him. I was eighteen."

He said, "The man looked at me and shook his head. He told me he wanted someone older."

He took time to unwrap a cigar.

"I hadn't been eighteen very long," Olney said. "But I had played three years on the high school football team, drove a car, wasn't afraid of anything. And like all eighteen-year-olds I thought I was pretty smart. I could do anything I wanted to do." He lit the cigar.

"He asked how old I was and I said twenty. And he said I didn't look that old. That I looked younger than that."

Olney said, "I told him that he, too, looked younger than he probably was."

She liked that, and laughed. Olney did, too.

"He hired me," Olney said, "just to teach me not to be such a wise guy. Really worked me hard. Accepted no excuses. Kept at me all the time. Called me a smart-assed kid anytime I did anything dumb. Made me learn to do things right. For twenty years. Taught me everything he could possibly teach me. One of the best friends I ever had."

He said, "At the old man's funeral I cried like a baby."

He reached into the cooler and got himself another beer.

"That's a good story, Olney."

"Thanks."

Then he broke the news that he was selling the house. But not to tell Cheryl or Heather yet.

"Why?"

He said, "I can't just sit here watching the scenery and taking Solomon for walks. I need to get out and get involved with things. Go places. Fall in love, or something."

They watched the green hills and blue sky some more.

Then Heather was there and asked DeeDee if she felt like playing a little one-on-one."

DeeDee didn't answer for a moment or two, as if her mind were on something else. Then finally said, "Sure." And stood up.

"Excuse me, Olney, while I go beat Heather at a little one-on-one."

"All right."

Olney said, "Keep your elbow in."

At the courthouse, Otis waited outside the courtroom on a wooden bench from noon until almost one o'clock. Then a court officer came out to tell him that the judge apologized for the delay, but it would still be a while before his case could be heard. Then about one-thirty a tall, gray-haired, tired-looking older man came out of the courtroom to lead Otis down the hall and through the door into the judge's private chambers.

The judge was a woman. Middle-aged, graying hair, tall, slender, and attractive. She wore glasses. She seemed friendly, serious, and at this particular time, tired. The official who had ushered Otis into the room took from her a paper she had been signing as they entered. Then she stood up. She and Otis shook hands. The official left and they were alone.

The room looked much the way Otis had expected it would look. Long shelves of law books gave a tone of solid authority and justice. There was a flag on a stand in the corner and on the walls large portraits of former judges in somber robes. Two tall windows, sunlight, flowers on a side table.

"I always handle adoption petitions here rather than in the courtroom," she said. "It's not quite so hard and formal."

She pushed an ashtray toward him.

"Please smoke, if you'd like."

He thanked her, but said he didn't smoke.

"Good for you."

She apologized for the delay. "We had two quite difficult cases that ran much longer than I had anticipated."

"It's all right. I don't mind."

"That last one was especially difficult. It will take me a while to recover from that."

"Sorry."

She was wearing her judicial robe, a dark gray garment. It did not make her look intimidating, but created almost the opposite effect. She was simply a goodlooking woman working at a difficult and exhausting job.

"Tell me your reasons for petitioning this court to permit you to examine your adoption records."

She took off her glasses and put them on the desk.

"You haven't had your lunch yet, have you?"

She laughed. "I haven't actually. Nice of you even to think of it."

She asked, "Have you?"

He hadn't. He said he wasn't hungry.

She put her glasses back on, looked more serious, leaned back in her large swivel chair.

"Tell me about yourself and why you feel you need to know who your real mother is."

He told about having been raised in Stockbridge and all the time knowing he'd been adopted. That both of his adoptive parents had been killed in an airplane crash a year ago.

She was sorry to hear about his parents being killed in an airplane crash.

Thanks.

"In your petition you said that your primary reason for wanting to locate your real mother was to see if she were maybe a person in need of help. Or to learn whether maybe she had been looking for you."

He said both things were true.

She swivelled a slight bit in her chair and looked at him. A small smile on her face.

"Would you have filed this petition had not both your adoptive parents died?"

He thought for a moment, then said he probably wouldn't have.

She nodded. That was what she had thought.

"There are a number of reasons why adopted children in their later years seek to locate their real mother. Death of the adoptive parents is the main one."

She mentioned briefly a few of the others, such as trauma, tragedy, depression, anger.

"It is always possible, of course, but not very likely, that your mother is in need of help and would benefit by your locating her. On the other hand, as all probate court justices know very well, disclosure of the fact that the woman once had an illegitimate child could be devastating. It might be enough to destroy her marriage, if she is married. Ruin her career, if she has one. Bring great unhappiness in other possible ways."

She said, "Many lives, not just that of the mother, could be seriously damaged just because an adopted child seeks to satisfy his or her curiosity regarding what kind of person their mother was."

She said, "This court never takes that risk."

She leaned back again. Relaxed a little.

"The paper you saw me sign and give to the clerk who brought you in here was the denial of your petition."

All right.

"I understand."

He said, "I'll get on my way so you can go and have lunch."

She appreciated his being so considerate, but said she thought it might be better if they talked a little longer.

"Cases of this kind are usually very emotional. Women weep. Men pound the table." She said. "Most people, after waiting a long time for a hearing and building up their hopes, feel a lot of tension that needs to be released in some way. So I would feel better if we talked a while and I was sure that you felt all right."

"I feel all right."

She said, "You teach at Berkshire Community College. Do you like that?"

He said that he did.

"You are tall. Did you play basketball?"

"In college."

"Young, good looking, and enjoy your work." She looked at him a moment.

"Things are going well for you, aren't they?"

He nodded, smiled, said, "I hope things are going well for you, too."

She laughed, said yes, things were going well.

"Are you married?"

She said she was. "Three children. The youngest one starts college in September."

For a judge, she was nice.

"Why aren't you married?"

He said he wasn't sure. That he had a hard time understanding women.

"I lived with a woman for several years and would have married her. But she said she didn't want to marry anyone."

The judge seemed more concerned abut him than he thought she would be. Which he didn't mind.

"Don't you have a girl friend?" Someone you like very much?"

"There's a young woman in the apartment building I live in who I'd love to marry. But she's about to become engaged to someone else."

He told her some things about the apartment building he lived in and the people. He told her about Olney and the kids and the basketball court.

"This young woman you say you'd ask to marry if she were not about to become engaged to someone else, does she know you love her?"

"I suppose not."

"You haven't told her?"

He said he hadn't.

All right. She nodded a few times. Leaned forward once more.

"Anyway," she said, "as best I can tell, you are not unhappy and depressed because you didn't learn who your real mother is."

He agreed with that.

She stood up, told him she was happy to have met him, was glad that he wasn't angry at her for denying his petition. And wished him well.

Otis said, "Maybe I'll see you around town sometime."

"That would be nice. I'd like that."

Before he left, she had one last bit of advice for him.

First, she asked if he would like to have it.

She said, "Would you care for some free advice from a woman old enough to be your mother?"

"Sure."

"As one who obviously knows more about women than you do, my advice is that you at least tell the young woman that you love her."

She said, "If you don't at least do that, you will regret it for the rest of your life."

Twenty-three

Pete's son, Ben, showed up early Sunday morning with the new camper, and Olney liked it. Just the right size. Not too big.

Ben looked like his father. Talked like him. Probably fished hard and swore hard the way his father did.

Just for the fun of it, Olney checked him out.

"How's the fishing over there these days?"

Ben said the fishing was no goddam good, but that last Sunday he hooked a pike in the Connecticut River that was at least three feet long and that he'd got it almost into the boat when. . . . And Olney was glad the kids weren't around to hear Ben's description of the moral, sexual, religious, and physical characteristics of that despicable inhabitant of the otherwise beautiful Connecticut River.

"Tell your father the camper looks like just what I want."

Ben said he'd do that.

"I'll call him tomorrow."

Ben said, "All right." Then he and his friend headed back to Northampton.

Olney took the camper for a trial run. Over to West Stockbridge, then up the steep and curving road to Lenox, back past Stockbridge Bowl, across Rattlesnake Road to Route 7, and home.

He parked the camper by the side of the garage and everyone came out to see it. Heather and Cheryl wanted

242

to go for a ride in it, but Olney said he couldn't leave now because Harry would be here soon.

Besides, people were getting ready to leave for Tacy Van Rensselaer's big party.

Someone asked where DeeDee was.

Olney said, "She told me yesterday afternoon she was going to have dinner at her mother's and spend the night there. But that she would be at the party."

What DeeDee had said was that she felt bad because she had not been spending much time there with her family lately. But Olney didn't feel it necessary to include that.

"She said she and her mother would go to the party together."

Brenda said, "You're going to miss an exciting party, Olney."

He didn't mind.

After they left, he got some beer and Cokes and ice from his apartment, filled the cooler, opened a can of beer, lit a cigar, and sat down to wait for Harry.

Tacy Van Rensselaer's party was scheduled to start at twelve o'clock. Lilly DeWitt was there by eleven-thirty.

Tacy, when he saw her, glanced at his watch.

"I know I'm early," Lilly said, "but I have a reason."

"Always good to see you, Lilly. I'm glad you're here."

Lilly gave Tacy a long look.

Already he looked like a state senator. Strong and handsome features and an expression that showed firm control of his own emotions and a critical appraisal of everyone else's. A little too overconfident. Ready to teach, preach, or expound on any subject anyone might show interest in.

Probably awful in bed. That was Lilly's opinion.

"Has there been a call for me?"

"No."

"I've been trying to reach Derek for days. I left word on his phone recorder this morning that if he were not coming to your party, as he promised you he would, that he absolutely must call me here at this number."

Tacy said, "I haven't heard from him, Lilly. So I expect he'll show up any minute."

"I need to see him right away."

"I'll tell him."

"It is a matter of great importance."

"I understand."

Tacy suggested she find a place outside and that he fix her a drink while she waited for Derek to show up.

All right. Good idea.

"I'll have a gin and tonic."

"I'll get you one."

He led her to a small table in a corner of the upper terrace overlooking the long stretch of grass in back, where the party was to be.

"Do you want to sit up here until the party starts? Or would you rather go down below to one of the tables there?"

From up here she would be able to get a good view of everyone and everything that was happening. So she told him she would prefer to sit here. And would stay here.

From the upper terrace where Lilly sat, a dozen steps led down to a long grassy area half the size of a football field, bordered by trees. Several long tables had been set up on the left and half a dozen adults, all properly uniformed, were loading the tables with plates, napkins, bowls, warming dishes, and whatever would be needed to serve the large crowd expected to be here. Charcoal grills were smoking, tubs were filed with ice and beer and soda, and one long table was crowded with wine and liquor.

There were two dozen small tables with white table cloths, and off to one side, not far from where Lilly sat, a short distance away from the other tables, was a picnic table without a table cloth.

Tacy brought her the drink.

"If you want anything more, ask one of the boys helping the caterers. They'll get you anything you want. Other people should be getting here any minute."

She repeated what she had said earlier.

"It is absolutely imperative that I speak to Derek as soon as he arrives."

"You will, Lilly. I promise you."

For the first time, Lilly had the feeling that likely Derek wouldn't show up.

She said, "Damn him!" And took a long sip of her drink. And watched Tacy as he walked down and had a brief conversation with one of the caterers. And had another sip of her drink.

Pretentious fool, Tacy. Pompous ass. But she had to admit that he fixed a good strong drink. And had another sip.

It was a beautiful day for an outdoor party. And she felt herself to be properly dressed for the occasion. A white summer dress, a widebrimmed hat with small flowers, dark glasses and a cane. The cane was not needed for walking. Lilly walked perfectly well without it. The reason she had brought the cane was so she could point it threateningly at Derek DeWitt, her womanizing young brother, and tell him precisely and positively what he was to say to his son, Charles, regarding Derek's blood relationship to DeeDee, the young woman Charles planned to marry.

Should Derek not say to Charles what any decent human being would say, that DeeDee was Charles's half-sister, then Lilly would feel obligated to rap Derek hard a number of times with the cane until he understood what he was to do.

Just for practice, she rapped the cane hard several times on the railing beside her, pointed it at a young man passing by, told him she wanted another gin and tonic.

The young man, black trousers and short white jacket, dark hair that curled down over his forehead, heard what she said, heard her say it a second time, and left to do as he had been told.

When he returned and put the drink in front of her, he said, "This isn't my job, lady."

She said, "Don't worry about it. Just do as you're told."

The large grassy area began to fill with people. They came around both sides of the house, but never in such large numbers that there was not time enough to tell which ones she knew and which she didn't.

There were not many she did not either know or know about.

A small group came and sat at the picnic table not far from where she sat. The one somewhat separate from the other tables. One of them was Lilly's friend, Brenda, the writer, looking nice in a pink dress and white hat. With her was a young black girl holding a basketball. With them was the young man, Otis Markham, one of the boys who had modeled for the painting. A tall and lanky young man who looked as if he felt out of place here. Which, of course, he was.

She knew about Otis. Knew who his real mother was. That was one of the secrets she would carry to her grave.

Those three were joined almost immediately by a slender gray-haired woman and a young girl carrying a sketch pad or something. The woman was Mary Ostrowski, who had modeled for the waitress in the painting. Lilly had never met her, but knew who she was.

She saw Brenda and Otis go over to one of the tables and bring back beer and soda and bowls of pretzels and potato chips.

In the center of the area a microphone and loudspeakers had been set up. Tacy would make his speech from that spot. Next to that spot a low wall had been constructed that resembled the low wall in front of the Stockbridge Library. The one on which the three boys had sat and watched the honeymooners passing by.

Ten or fifteen feet off to the left, what was apparently the original oil painting rested on a large easel. It was covered over by white cloth which, one would guess, would be taken off at the proper moment. The unveiling. Guarding the painting was a young police officer with a gun in his holster.

Officer Stanley Pointek. He had been on the police force only three or four years. The one who had got the youngest Thortner girl, Julie, in trouble.

He was a good officer. Julie Thortner could have done worse.

Would have done worse.

There were all kinds of people here. Judges, lawyers, bankers, politicians, local tradesmen, prominent businesspeople. Plus photographers and reporters.

Lilly saw Otis's mother, there with her husband and oldest boy.

She saw an older man who had once been her lover, years ago. He was there with his wife. An unattractive woman with dyed blond hair and wrinkles.

A casually dressed young couple, looking as if they had probably come for the refreshments rather than anything else, came close enough so that by rapping on the railing with her cane she could get their attention. She pointed out the boy in the black trousers and short white jacket, the one with the curly hair falling down over his forehead, and asked if one of them would please go tell that boy to bring her another gin and tonic.

"And ask him to also bring me a bowl of chips or pretzels or something."

The young woman offered to pass along that message. And did.

The boy in the short white jacket brought the drink and pretzels, put them in front of her. She said, "Thank you."

"I shouldn't be doing this, lady. I got other things I'm supposed to do."

She said, "Don't worry about it. You're doing fine."

Two men in their middle twenties arrived, wearing motorcycle outfits and carrying their helmets. One of them was Billie Cooter's younger brother, Jimmy. There to sit in for his brother Billie at his place on the low stone wall.

Tacy went over to give them a large welcome and a big handshake.

A newspaper reporter walked toward them to get a story.

Derek still had not shown up. And wouldn't. She knew that.

Then things suddenly got much more interesting.

Rhonda Mason, still a beautiful woman, came onto the scene accompanied by her daughter, DeeDee. From the picnic table, Otis Markham hurried out quickly to intercept them. The three of them huddled together for a few moments, then Otis led DeeDee a few steps to one side and from where Lilly sat it seemed as if they were arguing about something. He looked down on her, sort of shaking his finger. She looked up, standing as tall as she could, shaking her fist as if she would like to reach up and punch him.

"Why did you wait until right now to tell me?"

"Because you said you were going to marry Charles, that's why."

He said, "What did you expect me to do?"

"Well, you could have told me anyway."

"If you'd used your brains, you'd have known it."

He said, "Why do you think I didn't want you to marry that fool, Charles?"

"Because you were jealous, that's why."

"All right. So I was jealous."

He said, "Anyway, I love you. And I thought you should know that."

Charles, who had been talking to some people from Pittsfield, one of whom, Lilly noticed, just happened to be Otis's mother, now saw Rhonda and DeeDee and Otis and moved over and joined their tight little circle.

DeeDee said, "Thanks. You picked a great time to tell me. Right when they are about to announce my engagement."

Charles arrived with his arms wide open, ready to give everyone there, except Otis, a big hug. But Rhonda stepped forward a foot or two to stop him.

"Charles," she said, "I have some bad news for you."

He lowered his arms part way.

"DeeDee doesn't want to be engaged today. She wants more time to think it over."

Charles looked at DeeDee.

"Is that true?"

Rhonda edged a bit closer to Charles, and in a low voice, as if confiding something to him alone, said, "It's over Charles. Take my word for it."

"This is up to DeeDee, Rhonda. Not you."

"This is up to me, Charles. Take my word for it."

She said, "I can't believe I've waited all this time."

Rhonda took DeeDee's arm and led her over toward where DeeDee's friends sat at the picnic table.

Otis moved to the spot vacated by Rhonda.

Charles said, "I don't like this."

"That's too bad," Otis said. "I don't think there is anything you can do about it."

Lilly smacked her cane hard four times on the railing and got the attention of a short, gray-bearded, balding man holding onto a drink and looking with amusement at the crowd.

She spoke very firmly to him. She said, "Go to that table, the picnic table, and tell the woman in the pink dress I want to see her immediately."

The man, holding to the same look of amusement, laughed, shrugged his shoulders, said, "Okay, lady. I'll tell her. You wait right there."

Charles and Otis had almost reached the pushing and shoving stage. Tacy happened to notice, sensed that some kind of trouble was developing, hurried to join them. A few words were exchanged, then Otis turned and went back to his table. Tacy took Charles's arm and the two of them moved over to join the larger crowd.

Brenda pulled a chair up next to Lilly's table.

"What was going on out there?"

"I don't have the full story myself," Brenda said. "But it seems that DeeDee is in love with Otis, not Charles. She's not going to get engaged to Charles."

"Not going to get engaged to Charles?"

"No."

Lilly was not sure she was hearing this correctly. She took a moment to think about it.

"What were she and Otis arguing about?"

"Because Otis had loved her all the time but didn't tell her."

All right. Maybe that made sense.

In all of this, only one thing was important. Whether DeeDee and Charles still wanted to get married. So she asked Brenda that one more time. Just to be sure.

"No, Lilly. No."

"Then that solves our little problem, doesn't it?"

"Yes, Lilly."

They smiled at one another.

Lilly said, "Dear, would you do me a favor?"

"Of course, Lilly. Any time."

"Will you please go tell that young man in the dark trousers and short white jacket, the one with curly hair, that I want just one last gin and tonic. Then I must go."

She pointed out to Brenda the young man she was referring to.

"Of course. And would you like to come join us?"

"Nice of you to invite me, dear, but I think not. I'm going to have just one more little drink—then I must leave."

Tacy Van Rensselaer went to the microphone. He said, "One. Two. Three. Testing." He said that several times. A few people applauded.

He laughed.

He told the crowd that he was going to deliver a major speech later on, and that all he wanted to do at this time was make sure the microphone worked. And he made a joke about how microphones, like people, should work if they want to be part of what is happening.

"Everyone have a good time," he said. "Eat and drink and enjoy yourselves."

He said that later on there would be the unveiling of what was no doubt Norman Rockwell's greatest painting, *The Honeymooners*, which he was donating, on loan, to the new Rockwell Museum.

"After that," he said, "we will have a re-enacting of the painting featuring people who modeled for the original painting twenty years ago."

That got more applause. He called everyone's attention to his campaign literature on the tables. Then he said that as long as he was up here testing the microphones, he might as well mention briefly some of the things he stood for.

That was a mistake. He should not have done that. He should have waited until everyone had had a lot to eat and drink and would have felt obligated to listen to a political speech.

Political speeches are hard to take on an empty stomach.

He favored putting muscle back into the military and prayer back into the public school. He wanted to see a closer look at social programs that encouraged idleness and unwed mothers. He wanted to eliminate all government programs that could be turned over to private industry.

A minute or two of this would have been all right. But after he had talked for nearly five minutes, Otis finished his can of beer and said he no longer felt like sitting down on that low wall and having his picture taken. Rhonda said that she didn't feel like standing up and trying to look like a blushing bride. Brenda said she didn't like anything he had said so far, and wanted to leave before he said anything worse.

Mary said she wanted to leave, too, and told Cheryl and Heather she'd be glad to drop them off on her way home, if they'd like her to.

They tried to slip out quietly and not attract a lot of attention.

Twenty-four

Harry liked the camper. He thought it was just the right size. Said he'd like to get one himself some day.

Olney offered to take him for a ride in it, but then they decided maybe it would be better if they loaded the furniture on the truck first. But even before that, it might be better to sit down and have one beer.

So they did that. Sat on the deck and talked a while about life and things and Rhonda Mason.

"Still a beautiful woman," Olney said. "And a great person. I really liked her."

"And good kids," Harry said. "I took them all out to dinner last night. We had a great time. Lots of jokes and laughs. Rhonda said it had been a long time since she had enjoyed an evening as much."

He said, "We ended up going back to her house and playing cards with the kids.

Olney said, "Bring them all over some time."

Then he remembered. Harry would have to bring them over pretty soon or he'd be gone. He'd forgotten about that.

He didn't want to talk about it.

"Let's load the furniture."

"All right."

It didn't take long. They put the big overstuffed chair on first, then the rest of the things. And just about the time they finished, people were coming back from the party.

Everyone said, "Hi!"

Olney said, "You're back early, aren't you?"

"It got boring," DeeDee said. "We thought we'd come back here and have a party. If that's all right with you."

Otis said, "Sorry I didn't get back in time to help load the furniture."

"That's all right."

Then Olney looked around. Something was missing.

"Where are the girls?"

That brought on a small period of silence.

Finally Brenda said, "It was my fault, Olney."

"What happened?"

"I forgot you hadn't told the girls you were selling the house. DeeDee said she thought we should come back here and have our own party, and I said something about how everyone was really going to miss this place after you were gone."

She said, "It just slipped out. I'm sorry."

"They didn't want to come back to a party?"

"They said they didn't." Olney felt bad. Things inside his stomach shifted around uncomfortably.

Brenda didn't look too happy herself.

"It wasn't your fault," Olney said. "It was mine. I should have told them first, before telling anyone else."

He said, "Everyone sit down and have a beer or something. I'll go down and get the kids."

No one showed much party spirit. But they sat down. Otis got some beers out of the cooler and handed them around.

"I'll be right back."

As they went down the driveway, he and Solomon, Olney explained what had happened. He said, "I hurt two kids' feelings real bad. I got to go apologize."

Solomon wasn't smart enough to know one kind of walk from another. He ran in and out of people's yards, chased a squirrel around and up a tree, came back wagging his tail and happy as if everything was fine and all was well with everyone everywhere.

"This isn't that kind of walk," Olney said. "You should know that."

If this were just the usual kind of walk, Olney wouldn't be slouching along with shoulders down and an empty heaviness in his stomach.

Solomon ran over to where a couple of kids were sitting on some front steps, let them pat him a time or two because this was such a great day for a walk and meeting people.

If you're going to do something, Olney told himself, you have to do it even though it may upset other people's plans. You have to give priority to your own life plan. If there is something you have to do, then you have to do it.

He kicked a small stone out of his way and swore a little.

You don't change your mind about something just because what you are going to do will hurt people. Even though the people you're going to hurt happen to be . . . your two best friends.

He watched Solomon, who seemed to know where he was going, turn into the yard of the building where Cheryl's mother lived.

All right. What he'd say to the kids was that he hadn't told them because he had already changed his mind. Of course. He wasn't so dumb, he'd say, that he didn't realize how stupid it would be to move away and not see his friends anymore. For God's sake!

Mary Ostrowski wasn't feeling too happy herself. She was sitting there listening to two girls saying they were going to run away and not come back.

"We will, too," Cheryl said.

Mary said, "Don't talk like that. Everything will work out all right, believe me."

"I'll run away," Heather said, "before I'll be adopted by someone I don't like."

Mary said, "That never happens."

The girls looked at one another. It probably happens all the time.

Cheryl said, "We don't want to talk about it."

Solomon came running in, wagging his tail, pushing his face into theirs. They were glad to see him, of course. It wasn't him they were mad at.

Mary asked, "Whose dog is that?" And held out her hand so it could come over and say hello to her, too.

Cheryl didn't say anything, but Heather was polite enough to mutter, "Olney's."

Mary said, "Oh." As if that explained everything. Then said, "Not Olney Heebert, of course?"

The girls looked at one another. Olney Heebert?

Heather said, "No. His name's just Olney."

Mary looked up and saw him coming into the yard. Saw him stop about fifteen feet away. Move some hair across the bald spot, as she knew he would do. Heard him say what she knew he would say. In a loud voice.

"Why didn't you follow me?"

She stood up and said what she had planned all along to say.

"Smiley's, for God's sake! How did you come up with the name Smiley's?"

She braced herself for what she knew was coming. He would grab her and hold her tighter than he should. Almost crush her.

Which he did. Then they danced around in a short tight circle, hugging, mostly laughing, but she crying a little bit.

Which was all right.
The girls looked at one another and shook their heads.
Olney!

Twenty-five

Olney said that if ever there was a reason for a party, this was it.

Otis and DeeDee took Cheryl and Heather with them and went into town to the market on Elm Street to buy food and drinks. Harry went over to get Rhonda and the kids. And Brenda went upstairs for half an hour to type up some notes on what had happened today, because what had happened today was to be the last chapter of her novel.

Mary helped Olney get the charcoal grill started.

She said, "It's good to have my book back."

Olney stopped what he was doing and put his arms around her.

"It's good to have *you* back."

That made her cry a little again.

Mary told Olney she liked the camper. She liked the shower, galley, sink, dinette, and the queen-size bed.

"It's like a small apartment."

He said, "One thing you will like about it is that if the weather gets so bad that it's not safe to drive, you simply pull off the road and settle down for the night."

She said, "Probably, if you wanted to, even in the middle of the day you could pull off the road and settle down for the night."

He liked that. He said, "That's always possible."

He told her that what he had planned to do with the camper was use it to visit a sister in Indiana, then a brother in Colorado, then go out to California to visit his son and daughter.

"The daughter with the hot tub?"

"Yes. But you don't have to get into the hot tub if you don't want to."

"If I want to get into the hot tub, I will." She said, "I make up my own mind about things like that."

Of course.

He said, "We got some serious things to talk about, you know."

"I know."

"We got two houses, I got two young friends who sort of count on me, I got two cats, I got one dog."

"It will work out all right. It always does if you want it to."

"I want to do something good for Heather."

She said, "I have an idea. We'll have to talk about it."

He said, "Solomon likes cats."

"How do you know that?"

"There is a cat next door and he doesn't chase it."

She said that her cats didn't chase dogs, either.

Even though it got off to a late start, it was a great party. DeeDee and Heather beat Otis at basketball, Harry made coins come and go and end up in unexpected places, all of Rhonda's kids took turns sitting still so Cheryl could sketch them, and the hamburgers were just right.

Harry said he thought they should have parties like this more often, and everybody agreed.

DeeDee said, "How about next Sunday?"

"Good. And it should start earlier next time."

"Right."

Then Cheryl had to go home because her mother would be getting home from work soon. Harry had to take Rhonda and the kids home. And Otis and DeeDee borrowed the key to Olney's rowboat for a little quiet time on the lake.

DeeDee asked Heather if she would like to come along, and Heather said she couldn't this time. But you could see how pleased she was to have been invited.

Mary wanted to get home to feed the cats and Olney was going with her so she could see for herself that Solomon liked cats.

She said, "I don't have any beer in the house. So you had better bring some with you."

He said he'd do that.

He said to the girls, "I'm going up to Mary's, but I'll be back tomorrow morning sometime."

He said, "If I'm not here when you get here, help yourself to Cokes and things."

"All right."

"There's food in the refrigerator, if you get hungry."

They said they'd help themselves.

"And if a real estate lady comes around, remember to tell her I said I changed my mind about selling the house."

They said they'd do that.